# JUSTICE

Book Four

Kathleen Kelly
*USA Today* Bestselling Author

# Justice
## Royal Bastards MC Jacksonville, FL - Book Four

### Kathleen Kelly
### *USA Today* Bestselling Author

ISBN: 978-1922883216

Editing by Swish Design & Editing
Proofreading by Swish Design & Editing
Book design by Swish Design & Editing
Cover design by Crimson Syn
Cover image by JW Photography
Model by Roel Ross
Cover Image Copyright 2025
First Edition 2025

# DEDICATION

To
Crimson Syn
for letting me ride with the bastards and raise a
little hell of my own.

And to the readers who jump on the back and
hang on for every wild ride, you're the reason the
wheels keep turning.

Note For
THE READER

Below is a list of the other club chapters listed in this book and their authors.

In order of appearance:

Anchorage, Alaska – **JA Collard**
Durango, Colorado – **Nicole James**

## SEVENTH RUN

Barbara Nolan: Saving Blood
Katherine C. Kelly: One Night with the Biker
Nicole James: Paying the Price
Quinn Slater: Total Carnage
Elizabeth N. Harris: Soul
Verlene Landon: Infected by Virus
Crimson Syn: Tick Tock, Boom!
AJ Downey: Iron Hearts
J. Lynn Lombard: Trigger's Temptation
Letha Gene: Tater
K.L. Ramsey: Reacher's Ride or Die
Roux Cantrell: Hot As Hell
Heather Dahlgren: Surge Attack
JA Lafrance: Closing on Lynx
Ciara St. James: Tyrant's Salvation
Chelle C. Craze & Eli Abbott: SAC-RIFICE

Emma Creed: Wild Card
Posey Parks: Ruthless Obsession
April D. Berry: Defended by Bama
Shannon Youngblood: Kingdon and Kourt
Jena Doyle: Blood and Magic
Angera Allen: Next Level
Kristine Dugger: Another Life
J.A. Collard: High Stakes
Maria Vickers
Claire Shaw: Malice
Kathleen Kelly: Justice
Rae. B. Lake: Rage and Paradise
Kyla Orinick: Scorching Faith
Lila Grey: The Bastard's Lily
Kris Anne Dean: Ravaged and Ruined
Dani Rene: Blaze
Nicola Jane: Bully's Darkness
Elise Gedicke: Deadly Aloha
Thetta James: Nightmare's Battle
Elle Boon: Royally Hidden
D. Williams: Raising Cable

Royal Bastards MC Facebook Group -
https://www.facebook.com/groups/royalbastardsmc/
Website- https://www.royalbastardsmc.com/

# Royal
## BASTARDS CODE

**PROTECT:** The club and your brothers come
before anything else and
must be protected at all costs.
**CLUB** is **FAMILY**.

**RESPECT:** Earn it and give it. Respect club law.
Respect the patch. Respect your brothers.
Disrespect a member and there will be hell to pay.

**HONOR:** Being patched in is an honor, not a right.
Your colors are sacred, not to be left alone, and
**NEVER** let them touch the ground.

**OL' LADIES:** Never disrespect a member's or
brother's  Ol' Lady. **PERIOD.**

**CHURCH** is **MANDATORY.**

**LOYALTY:** Takes precedence over all, including well-being.

**HONESTY:** Never **LIE, CHEAT,** or **STEAL** from another member or the club.

**TERRITORY:** You are to respect your brothers' property and follow their Chapter's club rules.

**TRUST:** Years to earn it... seconds to lose it.

**NEVER RIDE OFF:** Brothers do not abandon their family.

JUSTICE

# Chapter 1

## JUSTICE

The engine growls beneath me, low and steady. Midnight air slaps my face as I tear down the coast road, throttle wide open. The faster I go, the quieter the noise in my head becomes, and somehow, that's the point. Drown it all out—the images, the memory of a woman with blood on her skin and defiance in her eyes.

*Jet.*

She wasn't supposed to matter. None of them were. We were there to get in, kill as many of the other MCs as possible, and burn the place to the damn ground.

But Jet was there with the other women, like animals, used like whores. Even half-dead, she helped the others escape before looking out for herself. Broken, yes, but the spark in her eyes said *not beaten.*

Now that spark is burned into my skull.

Twisting the throttle harder, the asphalt blurs beneath me, lights smear into streaks, and the roar of the bike drowns the echo of her soft voice. Sure, it shook with fear, but she has a proud streak. Most of the women we saved never looked us in the eye. Jet did. And fuck me if I didn't feel it like a punch to the gut.

By the time the compound gates appear, the engine's rumble is down to a purr. As I pull in, laughter spills from the clubhouse, music, the clink of bottles, and the voices of my brothers celebrating the end of another dirty job. They deserve it. We all do.

But me? I'm wired wrong tonight.

I park, swing my leg over, and stride for the clubhouse doors. Heat, noise, and whiskey hit me all at once. Creed has his arm around his woman, Reaper is grinning at some joke, and Highway is halfway to drunk. It's a normal night for the Bastards.

They nod when they see me, but I head straight for the bar.

"Beer," I grunt.

The prospect behind the bar doesn't ask questions. He slides me a cold one, and I drop onto the stool at the end of the counter. I don't join in. Don't talk. Just watch the bubbles rise and pop, one after another, until they disappear, the same as my peace of mind.

My brothers are celebrating, and so should I with another successful takedown, women freed, enemies crushed. But instead, I see her face every time I blink.

*Jet.*

The girl who refused to die.

The girl who's got no business taking up space in my head.

I drain the bottle, motion for another, and tell myself I've got no business even thinking about the woman. She's broken, and I'm known as a player. I'm the farthest from stable there could be, and Jet needs stable, but that ain't me.

And even as I lie to myself, I know the truth.

Something about Jet got under my skin.

And I've got no idea how the hell to cut her out.

# Chapter 2

## JET

Darkness hums behind my closed eyelids, thick and heavy. Every breath scrapes through a throat that's too dry, and every sound feels too sharp. For a second, there's nothing but confusion, then the scent hits. Leather. Smoke. Whiskey. Not the same as before. It's safer and warmer here.

Boots scuff over the wooden floors, a door creaks open, and a soft voice cuts through the haze.

"Hey, sweetheart. You're safe now."

Devil, the Royal Bastards president's ol' lady, speaks softly, her voice cutting through the fog. Gentle hands check bandages while light footsteps move around the small room. The calm she carries doesn't match the chaos tearing through my head.

Walls press close. The faint hum of voices leaks in from outside, along with deep, rough laughter and engines somewhere in the distance. *The Bastards.* The men who dragged me out of hell.

Memories crash in, jagged and bright. Metal cages. Chains. The smell of blood. Other women crying.

Then *him*. The one who helped to pull me free. Broad shoulders, leather cut, eyes like a storm.

*Justice.*

Even now, his voice still lingers, a promise wrapped in gravel. *You're safe now.*

*Safe?* The word feels foreign.

Devil returns with water and helps tilt the cup. The first swallow stings, the second goes down easier. "You're tough," she says with a small smile. "Most wouldn't be doing as well as you."

Tough. Maybe once. The woman who ran into gunfire to open cages died somewhere in that place. What's left is a ghost wearing her skin, a woman hiding from her past.

A sound outside the door snaps every nerve tight. Deep voices rumble, low and masculine. One of them stands out. Rough, commanding, cocky, familiar.

*Justice.*

The door opens halfway, light from the hall cutting across the room. A shadow fills the space.

No words come. My body reacts before any thought does, curling back, my hands grip the blanket like it's armor.

He freezes. Silence stretches long enough to make it hurt. Then a nod, slow and respectful, before the door clicks shut again.

Air finally moves in and out, and my shoulders drop.

He didn't come closer.

Didn't touch.

Didn't demand.

Something shifts, small but sharp. Maybe trust, maybe curiosity, or perhaps nothing at all.

Sleep drags again, heavy and reluctant. The last thought before it wins, *not every man who wears a cut is a monster.*

Some wear it to keep the monsters away.

Chapter
3

## JUSTICE

Morning rolls in on a haze of smoke and hangovers. Sunlight cuts through the blinds in the clubhouse like a blade, slicing through my brain and revealing the heap of humanity passed out in every corner. Brotherhood has a scent of leather, sweat, and stale beer.

Creed's voice rumbles from the meeting room before the door even opens. "Justice."

One word, sharp enough to sober the dead.

As I cross the threshold, the air shifts. Maps, notes, and photographs are scattered across the table, and Creed stands behind them, all authority and calm menace. Reaper leans against the wall, arms folded, watching.

"The women are all okay. A few have scrapes and bruises. Lucy's dad is seeing to them and said none of them have serious injuries," Creed says, pausing. "What was done to them is going to take a long time to heal. Some have family, but a few have asked to stay with us until they get back on their feet. These women are off-limits to every member of the MC unless they initiate an interaction."

The words land heavily.

*Jet is going to be okay.*

Creed shakes his head. "If that happens, make sure it's what they want. Make sure every brother knows we will not traumatize these women further. If they're thinking of getting their dicks wet, make sure the women want it."

"How many are staying?" I ask.

"Five of them." He scrubs a hand through his hair. "Justice, you did good out there, but she's not your problem. Keep your distance."

Every instinct fights the order. Creed is the president, the man everyone listens to, but the voice in the back of my skull doesn't care about rank.

Whatever the look is on my face, Creed points and says, "Jet's been through hell. She needs space, not you hovering. Let Devil and the other club girls handle her. You know she's got the touch, and Jet already trusts her."

Anger bubbles under the surface at his order, but the fact that he noticed me watching her throws me. Everyone knows I like the ladies. I like them fast, easy, and forgettable. *What makes him think she's any different?*

"I don't even know her."

Reaper huffs out a laugh. "You watch her whenever she's in the room. We all know you, brother, it's not like you to show such an interest."

A long exhale leaves Creed before I can tell Reaper to mind his own fucking business.

"We've got another problem brewing. A contact inside the Jacksonville Sheriff's Office says the Feds are circling. They're linking the takedown at the Crimson Wheelers' compound to us, calling it an execution. Word is they're gearing up to make an example out of the Bastards." Creed crosses his arms over his chest.

Reaper straightens from the wall, tension slicing the room. "We cleaned that mess up."

"Apparently not enough," Creed growls. "The Bureau's got whispers about Russian involvement. Lev Ivanov's name came up in connection with the port shipments. The Feds think he's using us as a buffer between his operation and the law."

My jaw tightens. Lev Ivanov is cold, methodical, and loyal only to his family. A man who'd burn his allies alive if it bought him a minute of peace with the Feds.

"If Ivanov thinks we're a liability, we're done," Creed continues, his voice low. "The Feds want to choke the supply lines into Jacksonville, and they're itching to pin something on us. Make sure Lev sees we're still an asset, not a risk."

Reaper snorts. "How the hell do we do that? He's Russian. Loyalty is just a business transaction to that bastard."

"Then we remind him business is better with us alive." Creed's eyes harden. "For now, lie low. No noise, no heat. Keep our heads down and keep our focus sharp. The last thing we need is a war on two fronts, one with badges, one with the Russians."

Every muscle coils tight. Orders or not, it's only a matter of time before Lev tests that loyalty.

And if he does, someone is going to bleed.

# Chapter 4

## JET

Sleep doesn't come easy, not in a place filled with sounds that remind me of what I've been through. Engines rumbling, men laughing, boots on wooden floorboards. Every noise sends a jolt through my body, trained to expect pain, not peace.

The small room they've given me smells of soap and fresh sheets. Too clean. Too kind. The contrast messes with my head. Monsters shouldn't live in a place that smells this good.

Shadows shift outside the window. Two men pass by, their cuts marked with a skull wearing a crown, its grin twisted and knowing, like death itself is amused—*The Royal Bastards.* The name alone should terrify me, yet something about this place feels different. Not safe, but not dangerous either. Just watchful.

A soft knock lands on the door. "Jet?" The voice belongs to Devil, the President's ol' lady, calm and steady with a trace of an accent. Australian or English? "Brought you some breakfast."

She enters with a tray before permission is given, placing it on the bedside table—eggs, toast, and coffee. Real food. Not the half-rotten scraps they used to throw at us.

"Thanks" comes out rough, more a scrape than a word.

Devil's gaze holds steady. "You don't have to eat it if you're not ready. Just means I'll feed it to Feral, he needs the extra calories." The faintest smile tugs at her lips before she sits on the edge of a chair.

Her calm radiates outside her. It's unshakable, motherly, and feels genuine. She's the kind of woman who has seen more than she'll ever admit.

Silence stretches, thick but not uncomfortable. She doesn't push, doesn't ask for details or names. Just sits there, sipping her coffee while the rest of the compound comes alive beyond the door.

With trembling fingers, I lift the toast. The first bite tastes good.

Devil leans forward, resting her elbows on her knees. "You don't have to trust anyone yet. But you should know, you're under Creed's protection now. That means nobody touches you, nobody questions you. You do what you need to heal, and the rest can wait."

Her words hit deeper than expected. *Protection and healing.* Two things that feel like fantasies.

I nod, small but real. "I don't plan on being anyone's problem."

"Good," she says, standing. "Then we understand each other." Before leaving, she glances back. "When you're ready to step outside, come find me. The club girls are setting up in the rec room. Might help to be around someone who doesn't carry a gun."

The door shuts quietly behind her, leaving the air thick with the smell of coffee and the faint trace of Devil's perfume.

Outside, engines roar to life as men head out to whatever business they do when they're not saving broken women. Curiosity prickles where fear used to live. It's a dangerous feeling, but it's there all the same.

Trust is a luxury, and it's one I can't afford. Still, something in this place makes the walls around my heart shift just enough to let the light in.

# Chapter 5

## JUSTICE

Night settles over the compound. Most of the brothers are passed out, or halfway there, and the air inside is thick with whiskey. It's quiet outside, just the hum of generators and the low creak of metal as the wind shifts through the yard.

A shadow slips past the row of parked bikes. Too small to be one of the guys or a prospect sneaking a smoke.

The faint beam of a flashlight dances ahead of what I think is a woman, shaky but determined. As I get closer, I realize she's wearing one of Devil's jackets and has a bag slung over her shoulder.

In my gut, I know it's Jet.

She's running.

Boots crunch against gravel as the distance closes between us. "Going somewhere?"

The flashlight jerks toward my voice. Jet spins, shoulders squared like she's ready for a war she can't win. Moonlight spills over her face, revealing haunted eyes and a stubborn jaw.

"Keep out of my way." Her voice doesn't shake.

"Can't do that."

Her grip tightens on the strap across her chest. "You don't get to tell me what to do."

"Not trying to," I say quietly. "Just making sure you don't end up dead in a ditch."

The muscles in her jaw flex, and for a second, a spark of defiance flashes across her face. "You think that's worse than staying here?"

"Yeah," the word comes out rough with more than a hint of conviction. "Here, you've got a roof. Out there, you've got men who'd sell you to the next buyer before sunrise."

The glare she throws at me could cut steel. "You don't know me."

"Know enough." It slips out, and I say, "You're Hawk's sister."

That stops her cold.

Her breath hitches, eyes narrowing. "Reaper told you?"

"Didn't have to. You've got the same look he used to get when someone told him to walk away from a fight."

Emotion flickers across her face—grief, rage, and disbelief all rolled into one. "He's dead because of your world," she spits. "You really think I'd trust anyone wearing that patch?" Jet's face is twisted in a frown, lips turned down, and eyes looking at me.

"Hawk died because someone broke the code, not because of the code."

"Easy for you to say when you're still breathing."

The silence that follows could burn the air itself. She's trembling now, not from fear but from everything she's been holding back since the night we found her.

"Creed said you could stay as long as you need," I say quietly. "No one's forcing you. But running? That's a straight shot back into hell."

Her chin lifts, tears glinting in the moonlight. "Every time someone said I was safe, they lied."

"This time's different."

"Why?"

"Because Hawk mattered," I say, stepping closer but keeping my hands where she can see them. "And so do you."

For a heartbeat, something in her eyes softens. Then, the wall slams back up. She drops the bag, her shoulders sag under the weight of everything she's survived.

"Just... don't make promises you can't keep," she whispers.

"Wouldn't dream of it."

She turns toward the clubhouse, walking slowly, every step looking heavy. The urge to follow burns strong, but Creed's words echo loud, *'Keep your distance. She's not your problem.'*

Maybe not.

But watching her disappear into the light spilling from that doorway feels a hell of a lot like losing something worth fighting for.

# Chapter

6

## JET

Rest is impossible after facing Justice. His words loop in my head, sharp as broken glass. *'Hawk mattered. And so do you.'*

No one has said something like that in a long time. Maybe ever.

The blanket does nothing against the chill that's seeped into my skin. Every sound becomes a trigger, a reminder that this isn't freedom, it's just another kind of cage.

Only this cage has warmth.

Morning creeps in slowly, a pale light cutting through the curtains. Coffee and bacon filter through the air, making my stomach twist with hunger.

Devil appears in the doorway, dressed in denim and attitude, her presence filling the room. "Up, love. We're heading out."

"Out?" The word sticks in the throat.

"Shopping. You and the girls need clothes. And Creed's brothers need food before they eat each other." She grins. "You coming or not?"

No threat hides in her voice, just confidence. The kind that says she's used to being obeyed without ever having to demand it. It's probably because she's Creed's ol' lady but maybe it's just an Australian thing?

A slow nod forms before my brain catches up. "Guess I'm coming."

By the time we hit the compound yard, the bikes are rumbling, and the brothers are gearing up for whatever business comes next. The sound crawls down my spine, half fear, half nostalgia. Hawk used to love that sound, said it was the heartbeat of freedom.

The SUV waits near the gate. Devil's already sliding into the driver's seat, Justice taking shotgun like it's his natural place. Lyric climbs in beside me, radiating calm. Behind us, two of the MC follow on their bikes.

Justice opens my door with a smirk that's equal parts charm and challenge. "Ma'am."

A frown forms before thought can catch it. "You're all about chivalry now?"

"Sometimes. Depends on who's watching."

"I'm not impressed."

"That's all right." His grin widens. "You're not supposed to be."

The Walmart parking lot is a concrete battlefield full of noise, motion, and people everywhere. Too open, too many escape routes, too many threats.

Devil's voice cracks through the tension like a whip. "Eyes up, Justice. We're not here for a bloody date."

Once we are inside, the noise hits like a physical force. Too many faces. Too much normal.

Lyric keeps close, her voice soft in my ear. "Stay with us, okay? We'll get what you need and get out."

Every aisle feels like enemy territory. Every sound, laugh, cart squeal, or the distant beep of a scanner makes my body brace for pain that never comes.

"Thought this was supposed to be safe," slips out of me before I can stop it.

"Safe's relative," Lyric answers, eyes scanning the crowd.

Devil laughs, tossing a pack of cookies into the cart. "Relax, love. These boys are just making sure no one messes with our discount deals."

The absurdity almost pulls a laugh. *Almost.*

Bit by bit, tension eases as Devil works her magic. She makes jokes about date night, jeans, and how Creed prefers skinny ones. Lyric teases her about it, and the two of them banter like sisters. For a moment, the world stops spinning.

Then comes the question that slips out without permission. "You're not owned?"

Devil's laughter fades, replaced with quiet conviction. "Creed doesn't own me. He loves me. Big difference, yeah?"

That simple statement shatters something inside. Love, freedom, choice, these things used to exist before they were stripped away.

"Wait, you can leave?"

"Anytime," she says. "And when it's safe, so can you."

A heartbeat passes before the next question. "Could I have boots?"

"Of course, if they've got your size." Devil grins, grabbing a pair off the shelf.

The words shouldn't mean much, but they do. Boots. Something that fits. Something that's mine.

By the time we load the cart with food and clothes, the edges of the panic start to dull. Perhaps it's Devil's laughter, or the way the brothers nod respectfully when she passes, or it's the warmth in Lyric's voice. Whatever it is, these women make it easier to be around the MC men.

Back at the clubhouse, the noise of bikes growling, bottles clinking, and music somewhere deep in the belly of the building greets us.

Devil rounds the SUV, holding out a phone. "Call your mum, love."

The words knock the air clean out of my lungs.

Fingers shake when they take the phone. Tears spill before my mind can stop them.

"Wh-why?" my voice breaks.

"Because family's everything," Devil says softly, slipping an arm around my shoulders.

Justice steps in close, his hand landing lightly on my shoulder. "Let it out. It's okay." His tone is low and steady.

My question comes out small. "But you… you're one of them."

"Doesn't mean I'm not human, and we aren't the Crimson Wheelers."

A watery laugh escapes me, half sob, half disbelief.

Devil nudges me. "Go on, before your tears short-circuit the bloody thing."

With shaking hands, I dial a number that hasn't been called in a year. The sound of the ring feels like a heartbeat.

"Mom? It's me… Jet."

# Chapter 7

## JUSTICE

Creed's voice cuts through the bar's noise like a gunshot. "Justice. Outside. Now."

The bottle is only half empty, but there's no arguing with that tone. Out back, the night is cool, heavy with the smell of fuel and smoke. Creed leans against his bike, arms folded, eyes sharp.

"Devil says Jet's been cooped up for too long. Take her out. Show her the view. Maybe some air will help her remember what it feels like to be normal."

"That an order or a suggestion?"

A smirk ghosts across his face. "You know the difference."

He doesn't wait for a reply, heads inside again, leaving me outside wondering what the hell Creed is thinking.

Jet steps out of the clubhouse doorway, arms wrapped tight around herself. She's wearing the same battered jacket Devil loaned her. Her hair is pulled back, eyes wary but bright in the moonlight.

"Creed wants you to see the city," I state, feeling as though he's pushing her too far, too fast.

"Creed wants a lot of things," she fires back, suspicion alive in her voice.

"Maybe..." the reply comes with a shrug, "... but this one's easy. Hop on."

She studies the bike as if it's alive. "Never been on one."

I climb on and smile at her. "Then tonight's a first." The hand offered isn't a demand but a choice.

For a second, it looks like she'll turn around and walk back inside. Then her chin lifts, and she swings a leg over, settling behind me. Light. Careful. Close enough that warmth seeps through my leather.

The engine roars to life, and the world narrows to asphalt and the hum beneath us. Streetlights blur as we tear down the coast road, wind cutting through everything that's been festering inside.

At first, she's rigid, her hands hovering, body stiff. But miles roll by, and the tension bleeds away. Her palms find my sides, tentative at first, then firming up when the bike hits a curve.

When we stop at a lookout, the ocean stretches black and endless under the moon. The city glows in the distance, far enough away that it looks almost clean.

Jet slides off, hair wild from the wind, eyes softer than before. "Why bring me here?"

"Needed the quiet," I say truthfully. "You looked like you did too."

She folds her arms across her chest and stares at the horizon. "Hawk used to talk about rides like this. Said the world felt bigger when you're on two wheels."

"Smart guy."

"Dead guy," Jet corrects, voice flat. "Because he trusted the wrong people."

"That wasn't on him."

She laughs, with no humor in it. "You sound sure."

"He believed in something worth dying for." The words taste like truth. "That matters."

Silence stretches. The wind whips hair across her face, but Jet doesn't bother pushing it away.

"He used to say the Bastards were family," she murmurs. "You really believe that? Family?"

"Every damn day."

Her gaze finally meets mine, searching for the lie. Whatever she finds there must surprise her because the fight drains from her shoulders.

"Maybe he was right," she whispers.

The ride back is slower. She settles behind me, closer this time. Her palms rest lightly at my sides, and every breath she takes seems to echo through me. The warmth of her chest seeps through leather and muscle, steady and real, anchoring me in a way nothing else has in years.

The road hums beneath us, wind whipping past. It's the sort of night that makes a man remember he's not supposed to walk alone. And with every mile, the questions claw deeper.

Why her?

Why this woman, all scarred, stubborn, and broken in ways I can't fix?

Jet doesn't belong in my world, but the weight of her behind me feels right. Like maybe for the first time, I'm not riding to outrun something, I'm riding toward something.

No words are needed.

The silence between us says everything I can't.

# Chapter

## JET

Morning seeps through the curtains, thin and golden, touching and bathing everything in its golden light. For once, sleep came easily. It could have been the lingering rush of the night air, or the way the world finally went quiet for once.

*Or it could have been* him.

The thought stings.

A deep breath fills my lungs, but it steadies nothing. The scent of sea and sand lingers, dragging me back to the ride. The roar of the bike, the curve of the road, his hands sure on the handlebars, and the ocean breeze threading through the night.

Something inside had loosened out there on the road. The fear didn't vanish, but it stopped ruling every breath. The world had felt wide again. Free.

Now guilt sinks in like an anchor.

Justice is part of this life, the one that took Hawk from me. The one that uses loyalty like currency and buries its dead in unmarked ground. But last night, sitting behind him, it hadn't felt like danger. It had felt like peace.

A knock comes softly against my door. "You awake?" Devil's voice is warm and sharp all at once.

"Yeah," comes my answer, rough but steady.

She steps in, coffee in hand. "Thought you might need this. Heard Justice took you for a ride."

I shrug. "Yeah, I guess Creed thought I needed air."

"Smart man," she says, smiling. "He's got a good head for people. Justice, too, when he's not trying to drown his ghosts in whiskey."

Her words make my chest tighten. "He's not what I expected."

"What'd you expect?"

"Arrogance. Control. The same kind of man who thinks women are property."

Devil laughs, setting the mug on the nightstand. "Oh, he's got arrogance in spades, love. But that man? He's got a good heart. Doesn't know what to do with it half the time, but it's there."

Silence settles again, easier this time.

"You've been through hell," she says softly. "No one's rushing you. But if you let the good moments in, you might find they don't bite as hard as you think."

Her hand squeezes my shoulder before she heads for the door. "Breakfast in ten. Don't make me drag you."

The door closes, leaving warm air and a stillness.

Fingers drift over the edge of the coffee mug. The heat seeps into my skin. Devil could be right. Not every fire is meant to burn you.

Justice is trouble.

Everyone can see it.

The kind of man my old captors pretended to be, right before they took me. I thought they were fun, charming. Sure, they were a little rough around the edges, and then they showed their teeth.

But he hasn't looked at me like they did.

And that's what scares me most.

Because part of me wants to believe he's different, that his hands wouldn't bruise, that his promises might actually mean something.

Trust got me hurt before.

So why does the thought of trusting him feel less like a mistake and more like the start of something I'm not ready for?

# Chapter 9

## JUSTICE

The garage is partially lit and thick with the smell of oil, rubber, and stale coffee. Tools line the benches, and the floor is a graveyard of busted parts and half-fixed bikes.

There's only one car in here, and I'm under it, trying to fix it. My hands move out of habit. I tighten, twist, and repeat, but my mind is nowhere near the work. Every time the wrench hits metal, it's her face that flashes behind my eyes.

*Jet.*

The name alone brings up a mess of feelings I don't want. The look she gave me before we rode back was somewhere between war, fear, and trust. It's been burning holes in my head ever since.

The sound of someone approaching breaks my train of thought. Looking left, I see a pair of scuffed-up boots.

"You've been in here since dawn," Reaper says. "Didn't peg you for the early-riser type."

"Didn't sleep."

He snorts. "Is that why you look like shit, or is it something else?"

The wrench slams down harder than I intend. "Say what you came to say."

Reaper laughs and lightly kicks my leg. I roll out from under the car I'm working on and look up at him.

He's leaning against the frame of a half-built bike, smoke curling around his head from the cigarette in his mouth. "Word is, Creed's keeping an eye on you. Says you've been spending time with one of the rescued girls. Hawk's sister."

My jaw muscles go tight. "Her name's Jet."

"Didn't ask for her name," he says easily, but his eyes narrow. "Do you remember Hawk? Kid wanted to wear this patch more than anything. Brave as hell, loyal to the bone. She's not him, Justice. She's fragile."

Getting to my feet, I place the wrench on the bench before I say, "She's tougher than you think."

"Maybe. But you getting close isn't doing her any favors."

The garage hums with silence. It's the kind of quiet that crackles, ready to turn into a fight if someone breathes wrong.

**31**

Reaper exhales smoke, eyes narrowing. "You've got a type, brother. Lost causes with fire in their eyes. Don't make this another one."

The words irritate me. "She's not a cause."

"Then what is she?"

No answer comes.

The truth is, I don't know.

She's just there, in my head, under my skin, in every breath since the night we found her.

Reaper takes a slow drag from his cigarette and exhales, the smoke coiling like a lazy snake between us before fading into the dim light.

"Creed wants everyone sharp. Our friend in the Jacksonville Sheriff's Office says the Feds are circling. They're sniffing around the Wheelers' burn site, and Ivanov's getting twitchy."

"Think he'll turn on us?"

"Wouldn't surprise me. Russians aren't known for loyalty unless it pays."

"Then we make sure it still pays."

Reaper's eyes narrow at me, assessing my words. "You sound like Creed."

"Creed's not wrong."

He gives a dry laugh. "Just don't let a woman make you forget who you are, brother."

"When did you start smoking?"

Reaper frowns, drops the cigarette, and grinds it under his boot. "Don't tell Lucy. She doesn't like it."

That pulls a smirk from me. "I thought nothing

scared you."

"Lucy does." His grin flickers, half pride, half-truth. "Woman's got a temper and a heart big enough to burn this place down if she thought I needed saving."

The sound of the garage door rolling open drowns out whatever comes next. Daylight slices through the dimness, catching the dust in the air.

Jet walks past outside, heading toward the clubhouse. She doesn't look in, but something in me watches her until she disappears around the corner.

Reaper notices and lets out a low laugh. "You're like a damn peacock, brother, always chasing the next shiny thing in a skirt. What makes this one different?"

The question surprises me, and I sigh. "Trying to figure that out." It comes out rough and honest.

He studies me for a long second, then nods once and steps back toward the door. "Just remember who you are, brother. Don't let this one rewrite your code."

# Chapter 10

## JET

The compound never really sleeps.

Engines come and go, laughter bleeds through the walls, doors slam, voices rise, then die out, and every sound keeps me on edge, waiting for something that never comes.

The others, Devil, Lyric, even Lucy, move through this chaos like it's normal. Like the noise comforts them.

*Me?*

It just feels like static crawling under my skin.

A week has passed since the ride with Justice. One ride, and everything inside me has been off balance ever since.

That night I felt different. The road was quiet, the wind was cool against my face, and he didn't talk much, but he didn't need to. I felt it in the way he rode and slowed down just enough, so I wouldn't feel scared. It's a strange gentleness from a man built for violence.

But that's what makes it dangerous, isn't it?

Gentleness from a man like him isn't trust. It's the calm before the storm.

The kitchen is empty when I step in. The smell of coffee hangs thick in the air, and the old floor creaks under my bare feet. Sunlight slices through the window. There's no one else in here, and I breathe a sigh of relief. At least I don't have to make small talk with someone.

A half-empty mug sits at the far end, the black liquid long since gone cold.

Justice is outside in the garage. I saw him there earlier. I could feel his eyes on me, but couldn't get myself to say hello.

Devil says he's harmless unless he's pushed. But men like that don't stay harmless for long.

The screen door creaks open behind me. My instincts kick in, fists tighten, and my breath catches, but it's only Lucy.

Reaper's ol' lady moves with purpose, a flower tucked behind one ear and a no-bullshit look that could slice steel. "Didn't think I'd find you up this early," she says.

"Didn't sleep."

She pours herself coffee and glances over her

shoulder. "None of us really do. Comes with the life."

"I'm not part of this life."

"Not yet," she says, taking a sip. "But you're breathing our air, eating our food, wearing our clothes. That counts for something."

The way she says it isn't a threat. It's truth, straight and simple.

"What's your story, Lucy?" slips out before I can stop it.

She smirks. "Reaper's story." Then, softer, "Used to be on the run. I was hunted. Our stories aren't that different. Reaper and the Bastards saved me."

Our eyes meet, and the silence between us feels heavy with things neither of us says.

"Devil told me you were looking for work," Lucy says, switching gears. "There's always something that needs doing around here. Laundry, kitchen, books. Are you any good with numbers?"

"I used to keep the books at a store I worked at. My brother got me the job," I say before remembering who I'm talking to.

"Hawk," she says quietly. "Reaper told me about him."

The name hurts less now, but it still hits like a bruise. "Yeah, he trusted the wrong people."

"Yeah," Lucy murmurs, then tilts her head to the side. She opens her mouth to say something, but the back door opens.

"Lucy, Creed's looking for you."

*Justice.*

His cut is gone, his T-shirt is dark with grease, and his eyes catch mine.

Lucy nods and slips past him, patting his chest as she goes. "Play nice."

He watches her leave, then turns back to me. "You sleep okay?"

"Not much."

"Still not trusting me, I mean, us?"

A humorless laugh escapes. "You're asking the wrong question."

"What's the right one?"

"Why should I?"

He doesn't answer right away. Just studies me like he's trying to read something written beneath my skin.

"Because we've got no reason to lie to you."

"Everyone says that before they do."

"Then let me prove it."

The words hang between us, heavy and dangerous.

I cross my arms. "You always this smooth, or is it just when you want something?"

His grin fades. "Want's got nothing to do with it. I don't promise. I *do.* That's the only justice I believe in, and I don't want anything from you."

The name fits him too well. It's not just a title, it's a warning.

A sound from outside breaks the moment—a shout, boots hitting gravel, the roar of an engine. Justice glances toward the window, his jaw tightening.

"Stay here," he says, voice dropping low before he heads for the door.

Through the screen, the compound hums to life. The Bastards are gathering, their voices sharp and low. The air feels charged, like a storm is rolling in.

Being near an MC is like standing too close to a live wire—eventually, you're gonna get burned. These men breathe danger, and no amount of kindness can change what they are.

Maybe it's time I stopped pretending I belong here.

Maybe it's time I faced my mother, looked her in the eye, to see if there's anything left of the girl I used to be.

# Chapter 11

## JUSTICE

The air outside is thick with tension. Creed stands near the gate, talking low to Reaper and Winchester. The look on his face says it all. This isn't some run-of-the-mill problem. It's bad.

I move closer, boots crunching through dirt. The morning sun is already hot, glare bouncing off rows of bikes lined like an army waiting for orders.

Reaper glances up when I approach, his face grim. "One of Ivanov's men got spotted on the docks."

"Jacksonville docks?"

"Yeah," Winchester confirms, spitting into the dirt. "Word is, he's meeting with a contact from the Bureau."

A cold weight drops into my gut. "A Fed?"

Creed's eyes are hard steel. "That's what it looks like."

The silence that follows is loud. The kind that means everyone is thinking the same damn thing. If one of Ivanov's men is cozying up to the Feds, we're standing in the line of fire.

"Why?" I ask.

"We're waiting to find out," Creed replies.

"He's probably been arrested for something and is covering his ass by handing us over," Winchester says.

Reaper nods. "Our cop is finding out what the story is. For now, we wait."

Creed turns toward the clubhouse, jaw tight. "I want eyes on every corner of this city. Winchester, reach out to the Khans and see if they've heard anything about the Bureau sniffing around. Reaper, get word to Lucy, tell her to keep the ol' ladies inside the compound until we clear this shit up."

Reaper is already moving, muttering a curse under his breath.

Creed looks at me next. "You've got connections near the port. I want you down there, quiet. Find out what the Russians are moving or who they're meeting."

"On it," I say, already turning toward my bike.

But the moment I hit the lot, I see her.

Jet stands near the clubhouse porch, hair loose, eyes wary. Devil is beside her, talking fast, probably trying to keep her distracted.

She shouldn't even be out here.

When her gaze catches mine, it's like the universe narrows to the space between us. There's no anger there, no accusation, just something I can't name.

"Justice!" Creed's bark snaps me back.

I drag my focus away, straddle the bike, and fire it up. The roar of my bike drowns out the noise in my head. Gravel spits behind me as I gun it out of the compound, leaving Jet and everything dangerous about her in the rearview mirror.

Cargo crates stack up like coffins waiting to be filled. Seagulls circle overhead, squawking over the sound of waves slapping metal hulls.

I park a block away from the docks, kill the engine, and move on foot. My guy lets me in through a side gate and goes back to his job.

The air is heavy with humidity. A few longshoremen move between warehouses, hauling ropes and shouting orders. Normal enough except for the black SUV parked too close to the edge of the loading area.

I slide behind a stack of containers and watch.

Two men stand by the SUV, both in suits that don't belong anywhere near saltwater. The taller one has got that Russian stiffness about him, with his broad shoulders, perfect posture, eyes like cut glass. The other looks like a Fed through and through, with a buzz cut and a cheap tie. He's too clean for this place.

When the Russian lights a cigarette, the wind carries the faint sound of his voice. I catch one word, "Ivanov."

My blood runs cold.

The Fed nods once, takes a folder from the Russian's hand, and gets back into the SUV.

*A bribe? A deal?*

The Russian stands next to the open window of the SUV, and they exchange some words I can't hear.

I pull my phone from my cut and snap a picture of both men.

Whatever it was, it means Ivanov's man is already making moves, maybe without Ivanov knowing a damn thing about it.

Slipping between containers, I go back the way I came.

The second I'm on my bike, I call Creed.

"Talk," he says when he answers.

"Whoever this guy is, he just met a Fed on the docks. Handed him a folder that looked like documents."

Creed curses under his breath. "You get a photo?"

"Yeah."

"Good. Send it. Get back here. We'll plan the next steps. We can't afford to be sloppy with this."

The line goes dead.

I text the photograph, pocket the phone, then glance back toward the docks. The Russian is probably still there, standing in the sun. Part of me wants to go down there, press him for answers, but Creed gave me an order.

I kick the bike into gear and tear away, my heart hammering harder than it should.

Back at the compound, the brothers are gathered in and around the meeting room.

Phones buzz, and a low murmur runs between them. The air feels thick enough to slice it with a knife.

Devil and Lucy stand near the kitchen door, tension written all over their faces.

Jet is nowhere in sight.

Probably for the best.

Because what's coming?

It's going to get bloody.

# Chapter 12

## JET

The clubhouse feels off today, too quiet in some corners, too loud in others, like the whole place is holding its breath.

It feels charged, like a live wire waiting to snap. Conversations stop when I walk in. Eyes flick away too fast. The laughter that used to fill this place is gone.

Even Devil looks restless, her normal fire burning low. She's in the kitchen, making something she calls a toastie. It looks like a grilled cheese to me, but who am I to argue with the president's ol' lady?

"What's going on?" I ask, keeping my voice even.

She glances up, that Aussie twang rough around the edges. "Nothing you need to worry about, love."

Which means it's everything I *should* be worried about.

Lucy and Lyric sit at a table with coffee gone cold in their hands. Both of them are tense, eyes fixed on the window like they're waiting for something or someone.

"What's happening?" I ask again, louder this time.

Devil blows out her cheeks, leans on the counter, and levels me with a look. "The Russians are playing dirty, the Feds are sniffing around, and half our men are about to ride out with itchy trigger fingers. You wanted honesty, there it is."

My stomach twists. "And if the Feds come here?"

"Then we burn what needs burning and keep our mouths shut," states Lucy.

It's said so calmly that it chills me more than the words themselves.

I move toward the back hallway, but Devil blocks me with a hand on my arm. "Stay put, Jet. Justice will be back soon. Let him deal with this."

"Justice?" The name slips out before I can hide the flicker of emotion it carries. "He's not my keeper."

"No, he's not," she says, her voice softening. "But he's the only one around here who looks at you like you're not part of the mess."

The clubhouse doors slam open before I can answer. Voices rise. Boots echo. The sound of chaos closes in.

Through the doorway, I catch a glimpse of Justice

in his cut and a T-shirt clinging to the hard lines of his chest. He looks like he's been carved from stone, every inch of him rough, solid, and impossible to ignore.

The door to the room where the brothers hold Church is open, voices spilling out into the hall. Creed's voice cuts through the noise, low but sharp enough to carry.

"Ivanov's man is feeding the Feds information. I want his name before the sun sets."

Justice nods once. "Working on it."

Reaper mutters something about the docks, about loose ends, and Creed barks back, "No loose ends!"

The words hit like a gunshot.

Justice's eyes find me across the room as I peek out the kitchen door. I don't look away this time.

He crosses the floor, and even with the surrounding noise, it feels like the air folds in on itself. "You shouldn't be here," he says quietly.

"Where should I be?"

"Somewhere safe."

"There's no such thing."

That earns me a flicker of a smile that doesn't quite reach his eyes. "You're not wrong."

The MC members leave in groups. Reaper is barking orders, Winchester tosses out boxes of ammo, and Creed is on his phone. The compound is coming alive, and it's not in a good way.

Justice's jaw works, tension in every line of him. "Pack a bag," he says finally.

"Why?"

"Because it's about to get ugly, and I'm not watching you get caught in it."

I cross my arms. "You think running fixes things?"

"No," he says, stepping closer, voice dropping low. "But distance gives me a chance to keep you breathing."

He's so close now, I catch a trace of cologne. It smells dark and clean. And damn if I don't like it. The scent sticks, curling through my head long after he steps back.

"Where are we going?"

"You'll see."

We ride for hours.

The sky darkens, heavy clouds swallowing the sun. The wind tears through my hair as I cling to the back of his cut, the thrum of the Harley vibrating through every bone in my body.

We pass fields, then suburbs, then city streets that feel too normal for what's happening beneath the surface.

Justice doesn't speak. Neither do I.

When we finally slow down, the sign ahead flashes familiar—*Greenwood*. The name makes my heart beat faster, so fast it feels as though it might come out through my ribs.

My mother lives here.

He parks in front of a weather-beaten house with peeling paint and curtains that have seen better days. Justice kills the engine, and the sudden silence roars louder than the bike ever did.

"Why are we here?"

"Because you need to see her," Justice says.

The words knock the air out of me. "You don't know what you're asking."

"I do," he says, unflinching. "You've been carrying ghosts. Time to bury at least one of them."

Anger flares hot in my chest. "You don't get to decide that for me!"

"I'm not deciding." Justice's voice softens, but there's weight behind it. "I'm giving you a choice. You've been trapped long enough, Jet. First, by those bastards who hurt you, now by your own fear. I'm not trying to tell you what to do or to save you, I'm here to make sure you remember you can still be saved."

The street hums faintly with cicadas and distant traffic.

He nods toward the house. "She's inside, she knows we are coming. Go on."

I glance at him, at the man who's trying to do something good in a world that doesn't reward it.

"You coming in with me?"

He shakes his head. "Not this time."

The words sound final.

My boots hit the pavement with shaky legs. Every step toward the porch feels like walking through glass.

At the door, I pause, hand hovering over the screen door handle. The last time I saw my mother, I was broken, angry, and ready to disappear. She had buried one child already. What will it do to her to see the other walk out of hell?

I look back, Justice is still there, standing beside his bike, watching, not pushing.

And for the first time since that night in the Wheelers' compound, I breathe.

# Chapter 13

## JET

The meeting with my mother wasn't easy. But after talking to her, there was no way I could stay with her. I love her, but I'm not ready to share everything with her, and she wants me to. We've been riding for hours, silence and asphalt stretching between us like an open wound. Justice hasn't said where we're going, and I haven't asked. I simply hold on, my arms looped around his waist, my head resting on his back. The bike feels steady beneath us.

The road winds through pine forest and coastal scrub, salt clinging to the air. When the highway breaks open into a lookout overlooking the ocean, Justice slows and rolls to a stop. The sun is sinking low, painting everything in bruised gold and red.

He kills the engine, and the sudden quiet roars in

my ears.

For a while, neither of us says a word. The ocean moves slowly and restlessly below, waves slamming into rock. He sits there, hands still on the handlebars, head bowed like he's trying to find something to say that won't make everything worse.

Finally, he breaks the silence. "You needed space."

"Is that what that was?"

"Somewhere you can breathe."

I climb off the bike, my legs stiff, nerves raw. "You think seeing my mother fixes what's wrong with me?"

"No," he says. "But it's a start."

The wind whips my hair across my face. I push it back and stare out at the water. "She knew me the second she opened the door. I saw it in her eyes... shock, disbelief, like she was staring at a ghost. She didn't say my name right away, just... stood there, frozen. Guess part of her thought I couldn't really be standing there, alive."

Justice says nothing. He doesn't move either, only listens.

"I thought seeing her would make things better. But it just reminded me of everything I lost."

He finally looks at me. "What did you lose?"

"Myself." The word feels too small for the ache it carries. "The Wheelers made sure of that."

He leans back against the bike, arms folded. "Tell me."

Part of me wants to stay silent. The other part is tired, so tired of the weight, tired of the fear. "They took me because of Hawk. My brother owed them money. He was supposed to make a run for them, but he never came back. They said he'd betrayed them. They wanted revenge."

His jaw tightens, but he doesn't interrupt.

"They dragged me out of my apartment in the middle of the night. Said I was collateral." I laugh, short and sharp. "Guess I was the message. Hawk died trying to protect me, and they made sure I knew it."

My voice shakes. "They kept me locked in that clubhouse for weeks. Sometimes they brought other women in. Sometimes it was just me. I stopped counting days. I stopped counting bruises."

I blink hard, but the tears spill anyway. "You know what the worst part was? Not the pain but the silence after they'd leave, and I was alone again. That's when I wished they'd finish it."

Justice's hands curl into fists. "They won't ever touch you again. Every last one of those fuckers is dead and buried. The Wheelers are nothing but smoke and bones now."

"A part of me wants to believe you... but are you sure you got them all?" I meet his gaze, my eyes burning. "At night, I wake up terrified. I can still feel their hands on me, still feel them—" The words break. I hang my head as shame floods through me.

He pushes off the bike and comes closer. "They. Are. Gone. It's simple. But you're still standing, Jet. That's something."

"Barely."

"Barely is enough."

Something inside me cracks when he says it. He believes it. And for the first time, I almost do too.

Taking a shaky breath, I glance at the horizon. The sun is gone, leaving the sky a deep bruised blue. "I can't stay at the compound," I whisper. "It's too much. Too many memories, too many people. I can't breathe. And my mom's a no-go too."

He studies me, eyes dark and unreadable.

"I'll leave tonight," I say, the words spilling out before I can stop them. "I'll figure something out. I always do."

"Jet."

"Don't." I step back, shaking my head. "Don't try to stop me. You say they're gone, and maybe you're right, but I can still feel them sometimes. In my dreams. On my skin. Like ghosts that won't quit."

"Let me help."

No threat, no order, only quiet conviction. And that's somehow worse.

"I don't need saving," I whisper, even though my voice shakes.

His eyes stay on mine, steady, unflinching.

"Didn't say you did."

"Then what do you want from me?"

"Nothing." His jaw flexes. "Just to see you breathe without fear."

That cracks something deep in my chest. "You don't even know me, Justice."

"I know enough." He steps closer, his voice low and rough around the edges. "You fight to survive when others would've given up. You think that doesn't mean something?"

"I'm not who I used to be."

"Good," he says, no hesitation. "Means you're still changing. Still fighting."

My throat burns. "And if I can't do it anymore?"

"Then I'll help carry it."

The silence stretches, heavy but not suffocating.

He's right in front of me now. The air shifts between us, charged and dangerous. I should step away, but I don't.

When his hand comes up, he brushes a strand of hair out of my face. His calloused fingers feel warm against my skin. The gesture is simple, careful, but it burns all the same.

For a heartbeat, the world stills. Just the crash of waves below, him and me.

I don't move when his thumb grazes my jaw. I don't flinch when he leans in, close enough for the scent of his cologne to wrap around me. It's dark, clean, and the scent is familiar now.

He doesn't kiss me.

When he finally steps back, his voice is rough. "You're not alone this time."

The words hit deep, deeper than I want to admit.

I nod, because speaking would ruin it.

Because maybe, just maybe, I believe him.

# Chapter 14

## JUSTICE

The meeting runs long. Too long. Creed is pacing the room like a caged animal, every step echoing in frustration. The air is thick with tension and stale smoke.

"Where the hell is my update?" Creed snaps, slamming a hand down on the table. "Our crooked cop was supposed to call two hours ago."

Reaper flicks his ash into an empty bottle. He looks lazy on the outside, but he's watching Creed closely. "He's probably waiting for things to cool down. Feds have been crawling all over the docks."

"Excuses," Creed growls. "We pay that bastard enough to risk a little heat."

He stops pacing, jaw tight, and looks between us. "Another source who is loyal to us shared some news."

Reaper straightens. "What now?"

"Hector." Creed spits the name like poison. "They swear they saw him down at the docks."

The room goes still.

Reaper frowns. "Is the source reliable? Hector is supposed to be done. Dead."

"They're someone we both know, and it seems Hector has risen." Creed's voice drops low. "And before anyone asks, no, he's not working with Ivanov. He's got a bone to pick with the Russians after what they did to Camilla. If he's back, he's not here for business. He's here for revenge."

I lean forward. "You think he's coming after us?"

Creed meets my stare. "I think Hector blames everyone who survived. Especially us."

That sinks in. Hector was Camilla's right hand in the Diablos before it all went to hell. He's smart, vicious, and was loyal only to her. She's gone, there's no leash left.

Reaper exhales smoke through his nose. "If he's gunning for Ivanov, he's bound to draw attention. Feds will follow the bodies right to our doorstep."

"It's why I wanted that cop moving faster. Now we've got a pissed-off ghost in our backyard, and the Bureau sniffing."

"Then maybe you call Ivanov," I say, before the thought can die. "Sit down with him. Tell him everything. Show him the photo of his man with the Feds, tell him about Hector."

Creed goes quiet for the first time, his eyes slide to Reaper. A look passes between them. Years of alliances, debts, and old violence flicker in that glance. They can speak without saying a word.

Reaper's mouth quirks into a half smile.

He nods slowly. "Not a bad idea." He fishes a cigarette from his pack, taps it on the table, then leans forward and lowers his voice until it's barely a whisper. "Let him come here. If things don't go the way we want? I'll gut him and leave him for the gators."

The words hang there, grim, final, and unmistakably serious.

Creed's jaw works, then he straightens and says, "Fine. I'll make the call. But we move smart. No heroic bullshit."

Creed's pace picks up again as he shifts to another problem like a man juggling too many fires. "And another thing," he says, voice tight. "Those women we pulled, Jet and the rest, are a liability. If the police or, God forbid, the Feds come knocking, having survivors from a rival club under our roof? That draws heat. That's leverage."

I feel Creed's words in my chest. "She's been through hell," I say.

"She's a target." Reaper's voice is blunt, unblinking as he leans forward. "You know what we should do. Drop them somewhere safe, hand them cash, and a bus ticket. Get them far enough away so they aren't our problem."

The suggestion lands like a blow. The room goes quiet, but the idea has teeth.

Creed holds up a hand before I can answer. He meets Reaper's stare, then turns to me. "No," he says firmly. "We don't turn survivors into strangers on the road. That's not who we are." He lowers his voice so everyone in the room feels it. "They stay. Under our roof. Under our rules. Extra watch, tighter security, no one out alone until further notice. We mitigate the risk... we don't punt the problem onto someone else."

Reaper snorts, displeased, but the edge of his reply softens when Creed adds, "If the heat rises, we reevaluate. But we don't do the coward's way."

Reaper sighs, irritated. "At least ask them if any of them want to leave. Tell them about the Feds, let them make up their own minds."

"And if they want to stay?" I ask.

Creed's gaze hardens, then finally, with a reluctant nod, he sets the boundary. "Then they can stay. But we tighten everything. No exceptions. If the heat turns up, we move to Plan B."

Later that night, the compound is quiet. I'm wired

after church, and I'm halfway through a bottle when I hear it—soft footsteps outside my door.

A knock follows, hesitant but steady.

"Come in."

The door opens just enough for her to slip through. Jet is wearing one of Devil's T-shirts, hair damp from a shower.

"I heard you," she says quietly.

My pulse skips. "Heard me what?" I ask, not rising from my position on my bed.

"Talking to Creed. You were defending me."

I shrug, trying for casual. "He's just doing his job."

"So were you." She moves closer, arms folded across her chest. "Why?"

The truth is right there on the tip of my tongue, but saying it would make it real.

"You've been through enough," I say instead. "You don't need the club turning into another cage."

Her mouth twists like she's fighting a smile. "You think that's what this is?"

"It's what it *could* be."

She steps closer until she's standing right in front of me. "I want to say thank you."

"You don't owe me that."

"Maybe not. But I wanted to anyway."

I can smell her shampoo, clean and sweet, against the smell of whiskey in the room.

She hesitates, then reaches out and bends to

touch me lightly on the arm, but it's enough to set my pulse off like a fuse. I stand and place the bottle on my dresser, take a deep breath, and face her.

"I don't know how to do this," she admits softly. "Trust someone. Be near someone without feeling like I'm about to break."

"Then don't force it," I say. "Just breathe."

Jet opens and closes her mouth, then says, "Goodnight, Justice."

She hesitates at the door, eyes flicking between me and the floor like she's fighting herself.

"Justice..." she says softly, "... stand still."

Before I can ask why, she steps in closer, close enough that the scent of her hits me, clean skin and something wild underneath. She rises on her toes and presses her mouth to mine.

It's soft. Quick. But it feels like the world stops moving.

Every instinct screams to pull her closer, to taste more, to take what she's offering, but I don't. My hands stay clenched at my sides, my cock goes hard, and the control it takes damn near shreds me from the inside.

When she pulls back, her eyes search mine. And I wonder if she's regretting the kiss, my lack of a reaction, or one hundred other things.

But I don't give her any of that.

"Goodnight, Jet," I manage, voice rougher than I'd like.

She nods once, lips parting like she wants to say something, then turns and slips out the door.

The silence she leaves behind hums like the aftershock of a detonation.

I drag a hand through my hair, my jaw tight.

She's a line I shouldn't cross.

And yet without trying, I already have.

# Chapter 15

## JUSTICE

The clubhouse is quieter than it should be. An edge of emptiness that feels wrong in the bones. The bar lights are low, with glasses lined up on the shelf. Only one table holds life tonight, Creed and Lev Ivanov, face-to-face, voices low and dangerous. The rest of the room is set up like a courtroom. There are four of Ivanov's men who flank him near the back wall, stiff and on guard. The traitor stands among them, appearing calm as he faces off against those who stare at him from across the room. Together we stand along the bar, Winchester, Highway, Reaper, and me. Nobody moves except to breathe.

At the back of the clubhouse, the med room pings in my head like a warning. Devil has Jet and the other women in there, waiting to see how this pans out. We all know there are charts, bandages, and Lucy's father on speed dial if things go south. That thought curls in my gut and sharpens me.

Creed doesn't smile. He doesn't have to. He's all measured muscle tonight, palms flat on the table, eyes cold as cut glass. Ivanov sits opposite him, suit too neat, tie too tight, with that Russian stillness about him.

Creed starts the talk. "Hector's been seen at the docks. A friend swears it was him."

Ivanov's jaw tightens. He fingers the knot of his tie the way a man checks a noose, and for a second, he looks human, a small crack in the stone. "Hector?"

Creed leans in, voice sharp as a blade. "We think he's looking for revenge after Camilla. If he's moving through Jacksonville, he's dangerous."

Ivanov's eyes flick to his men standing like black angels behind him. Ivanov clears his throat, fingers working the tie again.

Creed reaches across the table and slides a folder over, slow and deliberate. "We found this." He pushes it toward Lev Ivanov.

Ivanov takes the folder. For a beat, nothing moves except the light settling into the glass. He opens it with hands that don't tremble, and a single photograph lifts from the sleeve. A grainy shot, but clean enough, his man and a uniformed Bureau face, a transfer of something caught mid-air. My picture tells a story. Ivanov's gaze locks with Creed for a moment, then returns to the image and goes still.

He pulls at his tie and clears his voice. It's the only sign he doesn't feel comfortable. Lev's eyes meet Creed's when the sound of many bikes fills the air. Outside, the night is alive with the low rumble of engines as the Royal Bastards of Jacksonville ride into their compound. Headlights carve through the dark and reveal row upon row of bikes. Violent men straddling steel beasts in tight ranks of ten. Each bike faces the clubhouse, its lights shining inside, revealing every dark corner. The sound swells and then, as one, they rev, a single war cry that rattles the glass, then cuts off suddenly.

Ivanov rises, holding the photograph close to his side. His gaze locks onto the face in the picture. "Why?" he asks in Russian, low and dangerous.

The traitor blinks, confusion on his face. "I—"

Lev Ivanov's calm snaps. His other men move as one thought. Hands clamp onto the traitor's arms. One of the Russians strips back a coat and pulls a gun free. Ivanov turns to Creed, slow and deliberate.

"He will tell me what he knows," he says. There's no pleading in it, only a command.

Creed's face is a mask of stone. He meets Lev's eyes and shakes his head a fraction, not a refusal so much as a claim. Reaper is already moving from his place at the bar, the knife at his hip a pale promise. He steps closer, and the air changes.

"No," Creed says quietly, so the rest of the room must lean in to hear. "You can come. But we handle the interrogation. We don't hand over our problems to be fixed in your cellars. If you want answers, you come with us. We take the man to our warehouse. It's where we do what we need to do. You're welcome to watch. You're welcome to make suggestions. But this is our territory, and you, my friend, are in it."

Tension coils. Ivanov's men tighten their hold on the traitor. For a heartbeat, Lev looks at the rows of the Bastards' bikes blinking in the dark, at the shoulders and faces lined up, at Reaper's blade glinting like promise. He smiles a small, dangerous smile that doesn't reach his eyes. "Of course, my friend." He inclines his head. "We will come."

Reaper doesn't move.

Winchester stands next to him.

And Highway is a mountain beside me, silent and ready.

We move out in a slow, deliberate line. Creed and Ivanov slide into the Russians' Escalade, two of our bikes slot in front of the SUV, one on each flank, and two more take up the rear. The traitor rides in another car, with Ivanov's men riding point behind him. It feels choreographed, like a funeral procession with teeth.

The warehouse smells like bleach and death. It's a place built for interrogation, a metal table, a single light bulb hanging from a chain, the chill of spaces designed to make someone small.

They bring him in and sit him down under the bulb. Ivanov watches while Creed speaks, all business and menace wrapped together. The Russians stand a step back, like vultures waiting to see which way the carcass bleeds. I walk farther into the room with Winchester at my shoulder, boots soft on cement. Reaper lingers near the door, fingers loose on his knife.

Creed's voice is low and surgical. "Tell us what you gave the Bureau. Tell us who you met and why."

The traitor's eyes go wild, pupils blown in fear. He tries to shake his head, tries to look pleading. "I didn't... I swear. I thought..." His words die in his throat when he sees Reaper approach.

He'll taste his share of blood today before he gives up what we need. This warehouse has swallowed more than its fair share of men and secrets. Reaper works the old way with slow pressure, and the kind of pain that peels lies off like old paint until the truth shows up raw and panicked.

They strap the man into the chair under the single bulb. The light swings, and his pupils have gone wide. Reaper leans in like a surgeon and lets the knife show, an edge that draws a promise more than a wound. It's a threat carved in the air. *We will take you apart until you hand over all your secrets.*

Ivanov watches, hands twisting at his cufflinks. For a second, he looks fragile, like a man who finds the world less comfortable than he expected. Then, he snaps his hand out and backhands the traitor across the face.

"Why?" Ivanov asks, voice flat with no emotion.

"*Пожалуйста... пожалуйста...*" the man babbles, the Russian slipping out in a terrified whisper.

"What did he say?" asks Creed.

"He's begging, saying please."

Ivanov's face hardens. He stares at Reaper. Reaper smiles, slow and leveled, and takes a step forward. There's something in him now that's not human.

Reaper's touch is precise. He doesn't carve flesh for a spectacle but makes restraint an instrument. The blade bites close enough to make the man flinch, not to maim, but to remind him there's no safe corner left. The scream that breaks free is thin and animalistic. The chair rocks with it.

Creed steps in, voice low and controlled. "Why?"

"F-family," the man spits, voice frayed.

"We are your family," Ivanov says, cold as ice.

The man looks at his old boss, panic sputtering. "I have a daughter. She got picked up for..." He struggles, searching for the English word, then spits the Russian like a finality. "*Наркотики.*"

Ivanov looks at Creed. "Drugs. He said she got arrested for drugs." He studies the man, then bends so his face is level with his prisoner's. "Why didn't you come to me?"

The man's answer is a confession. "We weren't supposed to have children. It makes us weak."

Ivanov's jaw tightens. "My men don't have families," he says. "Leaves them open to the very thing this man has done, to betray. The men who guard me are paid well and are loyal to the Ivanov family and nothing else."

Creed's voice is gravelly. "What's his name?"

"Dmitri," Ivanov says, venom threading the word.

"Dmitri, what did you tell the Feds?" Creed asks.

The man locks eyes with his former boss. "I never betrayed you. I only told them about the MC and Hector Sanchez. He's trying to get back into Jacksonville. He wants revenge on you, Lev. I... I would never betray you."

Lev's hand snaps up and grabs the man by the face. "By talking to them, you betrayed me!" He pushes the man away as if he's something disgusting and turns his back. "Do what you must."

One by one, the Russians around Lev shift their weight and turn their backs on the traitor, a small, slow shunning that leaves him exposed. His head shakes in disbelief, and then he sobs. Tears mix with the blood on his face as he watches the backs of the men who were supposed to be his family.

Reaper moves into Dmitri's line of vision. "You will tell us what we need to know. In death, you will redeem yourself." An eerie smile creeps across Reaper's face, and I know at this moment he is lost to the bloodlust.

Dmitri breaks, he provides names, stammers out the contacts, where the papers changed hands, a meeting time, and a place. He tells us the Bureau man's name, the whispered code words. For every name he gives, Reaper smiles wider.

Ivanov watches the man disintegrate, and his face becomes one of satisfaction tempered with worry. "If Hector is moving, I will fix this," he finally says to Creed, to the room. "If he is a problem for my shipments or my men, I will remove the problem."

Creed nods once. The lines of kinship and threat are clear now. We are allies. We all have something to lose.

When we finish, when the traitor has given what he can and trembles into silence, Creed makes the decisions that stitch us back together for the moment. We take Dmitri outside. There's not much left of the man he once was. Reaper has seen to that. Lev Ivanov holds out his hand, and one of his men hands him a Glock. He points it at the back of Dmitri's head and pulls the trigger. This demonstrates to his men that he will not suffer traitors and proves to us he's willing to do whatever he needs to do to keep us at his side.

Dmitri's body does a half twist before it falls to the ground with a sickening thud. My ears still ring with the sound of the shot. Moving forward, with gloves on, I pick up one of Dmitri's arms, and Winchester grabs the other. We drag him toward the swamp and the alligators, who will eat the evidence. Their bite can exceed two thousand pounds per square inch, and their stomachs are highly acidic. By the time they are done, there will be no trace of the Russian.

When Winchester and I return, we see Lev Ivanov shaking hands with Creed. I can't hear what they are saying, but judging by the smiles, the Russians are on our side.

"That's good," mutters Winchester.

"Yeah," I agree.

The Russians get into their SUV and drive away. Creed whistles loudly, hand in the air, making a circle, indicating we are to mount up and go back to the clubhouse.

On the way home, my mind drifts to Jet, and I wonder what she thinks of me now. She must know what we've done here tonight and why. It wasn't only to protect ourselves, but it was also to protect the women who escaped the Crimson Wheelers.

The women in the med room are awake, and some have red-rimmed eyes. Devil stands guard at the door, her usual fire dimmed to a simmer. She's waiting for Creed, I can tell by the way she keeps glancing toward the hall.

Jet is the only one who meets my gaze. A flicker, unblinking, unreadable, passes between us. *Relief? Fear? Gratitude?* Hell if I know, but it hits somewhere I don't want to feel.

She lowers her head and slips past me toward her room. The click of her door closing echoes too loudly in the quiet.

I stare at the empty space she leaves behind, a dull ache twisting in my chest. This is why I don't get attached. Why I move from one woman to the next, never long enough for it to matter. My life isn't a home behind a white picket fence. It's here, with my brothers, built on sweat and blood. It's the only life that's ever made sense to me.

Jet is not built for this world. Not really. She's cut from something softer.

A hand lands on my shoulder. Lyric is standing there, eyes kind but sharp. "Go talk to her."

I snort. "And say what?"

"Everything. Or nothing. Just... show up." Her voice drops, quieter now. "She likes you, Justice. Even if she's trying not to."

I study her face, looking for the tell. "You sure about that?"

Lyric smiles, small and knowing. "She asked about you tonight. You were the *only* one she asked about."

Before I can answer, Highway slides in behind her, arms circling her waist. "This one's mine," he says with a grin. "Find your own, brother."

Lyric twists in his hold and kisses him, quick and certain. "He knows I'm yours."

Highway smirks at me over her shoulder. "Yeah, just making sure *he* knows too."

I shake my head, the corner of my mouth twitching despite myself. "You two need a damn room."

Leaving them behind, I head for the stairs. My

boots echo against the wood. Halfway up, I stop.

Every logical thought says to keep walking. But logic has nothing to do with the way her voice still lingers in my head or the way she looked at me as though she wants to trust me but doesn't know how.

"Shit," I mutter under my breath, turning back and moving down the hallway.

Her door is closed, a faint line of light showing beneath it. For a second, I stand there, knuckles hovering midair. Then I knock, once, twice, soft enough not to wake the others, hard enough to mean *I'm here.*

# Chapter 16

## JET

The door clicks behind me, the soft sound loud in the quiet room. Hands shaking, I press my palm against the cool wood, steadying myself. A wild drumbeat pounds in my chest, refusing to slow.

Tonight felt like chaos. The women who have been around the MC for a while were all ready with bandages and charts on the members of the MC who left. Devil paced almost nonstop, worry etched into her features.

And the only person I was concerned about was Justice. It feels like I've gone from one fire to another. From one MC to another. When he walked in tonight, I almost cried. He's handsome, strong, and I'm damaged, broken, and not even sure if I can let myself be with a man again.

I want to shut it all out. The noise. The faces. The

memories clawing up from where I buried them.

A knock sounds, two short raps, firm and controlled.

I freeze. *Justice?*

For a second, I think about pretending I'm asleep. But then I hear his voice, low and rough through the door.

"Jet, open up."

Swallowing hard, I twist the knob. The door creaks open, and there he is, broad shoulders and tired eyes. My chest tightens.

He steps inside, just one boot past the threshold. "You okay?"

The words are simple, and I could tell him how I'm feeling, but I'm not sure I can. Nobody ever asks me that and *means it.*

"I'm fine." My voice is too sharp, too fast. It's a lie.

His gaze flicks to my trembling hands. "You don't look fine."

"I said... I'm fine."

He doesn't move closer, just watches me with that steady calm that makes me want to scream and cry at the same time.

For a long moment, neither of us speaks. The air between us is thick with electricity.

Then, Justice takes another step in. "You feel like you shouldn't be alone."

Folding my arms across my chest, I back up a few steps. "I'm not some fragile thing you need to fix."

"I know," he says softly. "But you *are* someone I care about."

The words sink in, and I feel something twist inside me.

I hate it.

I need it.

I don't even know which is more.

Justice closes the door and sits on the edge of my bed, careful, slow, as though he can sense if he moves too fast, I'll bolt. He doesn't reach for me, only rests his elbows on his knees, staring at the floor. "I ain't good at this... saying what I feel."

I snort, the sound half laugh, half choke. "You? Mr. Broody, the strong, silent type? I never would've guessed."

His mouth twitches, almost a smile. "You think you're funny, huh?"

"Sometimes."

He looks up at me then, and I forget how to breathe. This kind of attention burns. It strips me bare, leaving nowhere to hide.

"Come here," he says quietly. Not an order. An invitation.

My feet move before my brain catches up. I stop a few inches away, close enough to smell his cologne.

He lifts a hand, slow as hell, and brushes it down my arm. It's the lightest touch, and my stomach flips.

"You've got nothin' to hide, Jet."

He doesn't know. He hasn't seen the scars, both physical and emotional.

My breath hitches, and I turn my face away. "Don't."

"Hey," he murmurs, fingers hovering near my hand. "You tell me to stop, I stop. Every damn time."

That right there, with the way he says it, hits harder than any kiss ever could.

I look down at him, searching for the lie, the manipulation I'm used to. There isn't one. Just him. Just truth.

"I don't know how to do this," I whisper.

"Neither do I," he admits. "But we can figure it out."

He leans in then, slowly and patiently, giving me time to back away. I don't. Justice wraps his arms around me and inhales. The flips in my stomach turn into acrobatics as I run my fingers through his hair.

Carefully, Justice pushes me back and stands. I'm so close to him that we are touching, his lips brush mine, feather-soft. Barely there. Then again, a little firmer.

It's not rough or hungry. It's *careful.*

And that terrifies me more than anything.

No man has ever kissed me as if I mattered.

I fist my hands in his T-shirt. His warmth seeps into me, steadying the trembling in my bones.

When he pulls back, his forehead rests against mine. "You're safe with me, Jet."

For a heartbeat, I almost believe him.

Then my past creeps in, the hands that didn't ask, the voices that didn't listen, and the bruises that took weeks to fade.

Stepping back, I hug myself. "You should go."

Justice studies me for a long time. Then he nods once and moves toward the door. "Yeah. But if you need me, you knock. Doesn't matter the hour."

Just before he leaves, he glances back. "I ain't like them, Jet. You'll see that one day."

The door closes behind him, soft and final.

I sink onto the bed, touching my lips, still tasting him there.

And for the first time in a long damn while, I let myself hope.

# Chapter 17

## JUSTICE

Sleep doesn't come easily, but tonight it's worse. Every time I close my eyes, I see her face, the fear, the way she trembled when I touched her, and the way she kissed me back, even though I know it scared her to death.

I'm not proud of wanting her, not after what she's been through.

But it's not just wanting, it's something else. Something I don't have a name for.

The clock on the wall ticks past one a.m. I'm sitting on the edge of the bed, boots still on, when a soft knock breaks the silence.

One. Two. Hesitant.

I'm at the door in two strides. When I open it, she's there, barefoot, hair messy, wearing one of those oversized tees that swallow her entire frame.

Her eyes look huge in the dim light of the hallway.

"Jet." Her name comes out rough, scraped from somewhere deep. "You okay?"

She swallows. "Can I come in?"

I nod and step aside.

She moves past me, arms folded tight, shoulders trembling. I close the door and lean against it, giving her space.

"Couldn't sleep," she murmurs, voice shaking. "Every time I close my eyes, I see... *them.*"

Her breath hitches, and I know she's fighting not to fall apart.

"Sit," I tell her, keeping my tone low, steady. I move to the edge of the bed, keeping my distance. She sits, and I settle beside her, close enough that her warmth seeps into my skin.

For a while, neither of us says anything.

Then she whispers, "I don't want to be scared anymore, Justice."

My chest tightens. "You don't need to be, not while I'm around."

She shakes her head. "That's not what I mean." Her eyes meet mine, raw and vulnerable. "I want to *feel safe again.* I want to remember what it's like to be touched and n-not..." Her voice cracks. "Not panic."

I drag a hand down my face, trying to steady the storm inside me. "Jet..."

"I trust you," she says quietly. "I just... need to try."

Her words sink in as I dare to hope what I think Jet means. No more nights thinking about what it would be like to touch her, to feel her beneath me. I don't move. I don't breathe. Because this isn't about sex, it's about so much more for her and me.

"Okay," I murmur, slowly reaching for her hand, giving her time to pull away. She doesn't. Her fingers slide into mine, hesitant but sure.

"Tell me what's okay," I say.

She nods. "Don't move too fast."

Smiling at her, I say, "Never do."

We start with her hand resting against my chest, over my heartbeat. I keep my palm flat against hers so she can feel it. "No one's gonna hurt you again."

Her breath steadies, and the tremor in her fingers eases a little.

When she leans in, I don't take over. I let her set the pace. Her lips brush mine, softly. I match her, keeping it gentle.

No dominance. No control. Only connection.

She shifts closer, climbing onto my lap, trembling but determined. I wrap my arms around her waist, holding her carefully, like she's made of glass.

Her forehead presses against mine. "I can't tell if I'm shaking because I'm scared or because I want this."

"Doesn't matter," I whisper. "We'll stop anytime you say."

She shakes her head. "Don't stop."

So we move slowly. Clothes stay mostly on, touches are light, everything is about *her and what she needs.*

It's not about taking but about giving and letting her feel wanted without fear.

When she finally exhales, her body relaxing against me, I realize she's not trembling anymore.

With care, I reach down and pull my T-shirt over my head. Jet's fingers trail across the tattoos marking my chest, tracing lines of ink and old stories. The touch is light, hesitant, like she's learning me by memory.

Leaning forward, I press a kiss to her neck. Jet exhales a shaky sigh.

Smiling, I do it again. She rocks against me, and my cock strains against the confines of my jeans.

I grip her ass and stand, taking her with me.

Jet's feet hit the floor, and she goes completely still.

"It's okay, Jet," I murmur, my voice low against her ear. "It's me. I will not hurt you. *Ever.*"

She nods, but I feel the trembling return.

"Let me make you feel good," I whisper.

My hands drift down her arms, light as breath, until they find the hem of her T-shirt. I lean in and kiss her, soft at first, testing, then deeper when she parts her lips. My tongue brushes hers, and she gasps, arms looping around my neck as she melts into me.

No woman has ever responded to me like this. The mix of fear and want, strength and surrender, does something raw to my insides.

While her mouth moves with mine, I ease the T-shirt over her head, tossing it aside before she can second-guess herself. Then I crush her against my chest, keeping her close so she doesn't have time to panic or pull away.

Her eyes are wide when I draw back just enough to see her. I tilt her chin and kiss her again.

It takes only a heartbeat before she presses into me, body to body, breath to breath, and when she does, Jet comes alive in my arms.

Her fingers dig into my back, and a hiss of pleasure escapes me before I can stop it. But this isn't about me. This is all about Jet and helping her trust what touch can feel like again.

Her breasts press against my chest, soft and warm, and as my hands roam the curve of her waist, it hits me—*she's naked.*

"Jet?"

"Mm-hmm?" Her voice is small, hazy with nerves and something sweeter.

"One of us is wearing too many clothes, and it's not you."

Jet lets out a giggle. It's light, unexpected, and the

sound cracks open something in my chest I didn't know I'd locked away.

"Can you..." she pauses, biting her lip, "... close your eyes?"

Leaning back, I study her face, the flush on her cheeks, the fear she's trying to hide. "Why?"

She swallows hard. "I'm not ready for you to see me."

"Right, right. Yeah, of course."

I shut my eyes. Jet's breath brushes my skin an instant before her lips do. She kisses my chest right over where my heart is racing like a damn engine on redline. The soft press of her mouth sends a shiver through me, and then she does it again, slower this time, her breath warm against my skin.

Then the heat of her body is gone.

I fight the urge to open my eyes, to find her, but I hear her move—bare feet on the floor, the soft creak of the bedsprings as she climbs onto it.

"Justice," she whispers.

"Yeah?"

"Open your eyes."

I do.

She's in my bed, sheets pulled up to her chin, hair falling wild around her face. Moonlight slips through the blinds, silvering her skin. She looks small and brave all at once, a contradiction that punches the air from my lungs.

"Jesus, Jet," I murmur, raking a hand through my

hair. "You trying to kill me?"

Her mouth curves just enough to tease. "Not tonight."

Moving closer, I slow, sitting on the edge of the mattress. The springs dip beneath my weight, and for a heartbeat, we just look at each other—the biker and the broken girl who doesn't realize she's the strongest one in the room.

"Still okay?" I ask.

She nods, the sheet rustling as she breathes. "As long as it's you."

Bending down, I tug off my boots and kick them aside. The room is quiet except for the steady rhythm of our breathing.

When I straighten, she's still watching me, eyes wide and unblinking.

Slowly, I unbuckle my belt. The soft *clink* of metal sounds loud in the silence. Then, I undo my jeans, pushing them down my legs.

Her gaze never leaves mine. Not once.

I should feel exposed. Hell, I *do,* but when a shy smile curves her lips, the worry twisting in my gut eases. That smile tells me she's still here, still with me.

Pride swells in my chest. Jet is being so damn brave, facing her fear head-on.

And in this moment, I know she's stronger than she thinks, and I'd burn the world down before I *ever* let anyone break her again.

"I want to see you," I whisper.

Jet's fingers tighten around the sheet, knuckles white. For a second, I think she'll tell me no. Then she nods slightly, trembles, and then closes her eyes.

Carefully, I grip the edge of the sheet and ease it down, slow enough for her to stop me if she needs to.

My breath leaves my lungs.

More than a dozen cigarette burns mark her ribs, and a thin scar cuts across her stomach, pale against her skin.

Rage flickers hot in my chest, but I shove it down. This moment isn't about *my* anger. It's about *her* bravery.

Despite the damage carved into her, she's beautiful. Maybe more because of it. Every mark tells me she survived.

I swallow hard and meet her closed eyes. "You're perfect, Jet. Every damn inch."

Her eyes fly open, locking onto mine, wide and uncertain. She's searching my face as if needing to know I mean what I say, if I still see her the same now that I've seen everything.

Holding her gaze, I don't flinch or show pity.

My hand trembles as I reach out, hovering over her stomach before I finally let my fingertips brush her skin.

She twitches, just barely, and I stop.

"Still okay?" I murmur.

Her lips part, and after a long moment, she nods. "Yes... don't stop."

I trace the scars slowly and gently, memorizing every ridge and hollow. "They hurt you," I whisper, voice low, almost a growl.

"They don't get to anymore," she says softly, eyes still closed.

That simple sentence makes my heart beat a little faster.

Leaning down, I press my lips to one burn on her ribs. Then another. Each kiss is a promise that I will worship her.

Her breath catches, and her hands find my shoulders, holding on like she's afraid to fall apart.

"You don't have to hide from me, Jet," I tell her, moving up to kiss the hollow of her throat. "Not ever."

Her eyes open again, glassy but fierce. "You make it sound easy."

"It's not," I admit, brushing a strand of hair from her face. "But I'll be here every time you need to remember you're more than what they did."

She lets out a shaky breath and cups my jaw. "Why are you so gentle with me?"

"Because you deserve it."

The smallest smile ghosts across her lips, and I know I've done something right, something that matters.

Jet's body fits against mine as if it belongs there, and every sigh, every tremor is a piece of her taking herself back.

She sets the pace, never taking more than she gives. My hands stay on her sides. I don't want to frighten her.

When she whispers my name, it's not fear or pain this time, it's trust.

And I know, without a doubt, this is what healing looks like.

Feeling bolder, I lay between her legs, my cock near her entrance, but I don't slide in. This isn't about me taking what I want but giving Jet what she needs.

Lifting, I kiss my way down her body. Jet shivers and gasps when my tongue slides between her folds. Her body arches, and her hands tangle in my hair. Gently, I suck on her clit, and she rocks her hips as I set the pace. Jet uses my face, spreading her legs wider, her breathing ragged. I slide two fingers inside her and stroke as my tongue flicks against her clit.

"Justice!"

My name sounds like a prayer on her lips as she arches up, and I press my fingers in deeper. Jet grinds into my face as I suck on her nub, and then I feel the pulses of her orgasm. Her body contracts around my fingers, so I lap and suck until every tremor leaves her body.

"That felt so good," Jet purrs.

Slowly, I kiss my way up her body, tasting her skin. When I reach her lips, I press a soft kiss there, a promise more than a claim, then roll to the side to lie beside her.

My hand comes to rest on her breast, protective, but still possessive enough to feel real.

"What are you doing?" Jet asks, her voice small, curious.

"Watching you," I murmur. "You're so fucking beautiful."

Jet turns her head toward me, eyes searching. "But you didn't finish."

I brush my thumb across her collarbone and smile faintly. "That's okay," I whisper. "Tonight wasn't about that."

Jet shakes her head and slides over me, my cock between her folds.

"You don't have to," I say, with my hands on her hips so she can't move.

Jet leans down, her breasts swaying, and whispers in my ear, "But I want to."

She rises, grabs my cock, and slowly slides down until she's taken all of me.

"Fuck!" I hiss through gritted teeth.

Jet smiles and rolls her hips.

My hands move her, and I want to be gentle. I want this to be about her, but fuck me, she feels so good.

She sets the pace, and I watch her as she closes her eyes, neck arched as she rides me. Nothing has ever looked so fucking sexy.

"Jet," I groan. "Let me move you faster."

Her eyes open, and my cock is so hard, I know I won't last long. Thrusting up, so I'm inside her as far as I can go, I dig my fingers into her hips and move her. Jet's breathing becomes ragged, and as I press on her clit, she moans out my name.

The pressure of being inside her tight, slick pussy, seeing her ride me and shatter on my cock brings me to the edge. My balls tingle, and I thrust into her once, twice, three times, then come undone.

This woman is addictive.

This woman is *mine*.

And I hope she knows I am hers.

Morning creeps in pale and cold through the blinds.

Jet is tangled against me, head on my chest, her breath warm on my skin. I've got one arm under her, the other draped protectively around her waist.

I don't move.

I barely breathe.

Because if I do, I might break whatever fragile peace we've found.

Her lashes flutter, then she's awake and instantly tense. She jerks upright, heart hammering, eyes wild until she sees me.

"It's okay," I murmur, voice low. "You're safe."

Color creeps into her cheeks, shame trying to take root where it doesn't belong.

Jet looks down, then back at me. "I... I didn't mean to fall asleep."

"You needed it." I reach across to the nightstand, grab the mug I made earlier, and hand it to her. "Coffee."

She hesitates, then takes it, our fingers brushing. "Thanks."

"Don't thank me," I say softly. "You don't owe me a damn thing."

Her lip trembles, but she hides it behind a sip. "You're too good to me."

I huff out a laugh. "You don't know me very well then, and that coffee is probably cold."

That earns a small smile, quick and fleeting but real.

Silence stretches between us.

Then she says, almost to herself, "For the first time in years, I feel... human."

I reach out, my thumb brushing her knuckles. "You *are* human, Jet. Stronger than most."

She looks at me then, eyes glassy, and whispers,

"Don't make me regret this."

"Not a chance," I promise. "You've got my word, my loyalty… and maybe more than that."

Her laugh is shaky. "Careful, Justice. That almost sounded like feelings."

I grin. "Yeah, don't tell anyone. You'll ruin my reputation."

Her smile lingers a little longer this time, and something eases inside me.

Whatever this is, whatever we're becoming, it's worth the risk.

Because she deserves a man who doesn't take.

And I'm done being the man who breaks things he cares about.

# Chapter 18

## JUSTICE

The world feels different in the morning.

Jet is asleep, tangled in my sheets, and the faint rise and fall of her chest soothes me. For a guy like me, peace isn't something that lasts, but for her, I hope it does.

Sliding out of bed, I pull on my jeans and cut, pausing just long enough to look at her again. She appears small and breakable, but after last night, I now know better.

I leave her sleeping and head for the yard.

The compound hums low with morning noise, coffee brewing, brothers moving, and the laughter of the women in the kitchen. Creed is standing near the gate, talking with Lyric.

"Morning," I say as I get closer to them.

Creed's eyes cut to me. "You see, Ronan?"

"The new prospect?" I blow out smoke. "Not since last night. Why?"

"Because I told him to do a simple supply run, and he's been gone for over two hours. No answer on his burner either."

That sits wrong in my gut. Ronan is green, but not stupid. He's been itching to prove himself since the day he patched in.

"Maybe his bike broke down?" I say, though even as I do, it doesn't sound right.

Lyric shakes his head. "No chance. He was seen talking to someone in town last night. A guy with Reaper ink on his neck."

"You sure?" I ask.

"Yes. After things calmed down, I went back to Dad's house. I stopped at the diner on St. Johns Avenue to get a late-night coffee and something sweet. He was across the street talking."

"Fuck," Creed mutters. "You think he sold us out?"

"If he did, I'll find out."

Before Creed can respond, Devil bursts out of the clubhouse.

"Creed!" Devil's shout slices through the morning quiet. "We've got a man down at the back gate!"

The three of us move fast. Gravel crunches under our boots when we hit the yard. From the gate, I see two of our guys dragging someone between them.

"Who is it?" Creed barks, already running ahead.

"Not sure," Devil answers, breathing hard. "Found him on the service road. He barely made it here."

We reach them just as they lower him to the ground. He's pale, half-conscious, his cut is shredded, and his face is a mess of blood and road grit.

"Jesus Christ," I mutter, kneeling beside him. "What the hell happened?"

He coughs, blood flecking his lips. "Rivet Knights... ambushed me on the way to see you. They knew I was comin'." Another cough racks his chest. "Name's Blake. I was sent from Anchorage by Sparky. Told me to warn you about the Rivet Knights." He gives a rough laugh that turns into a wince. "Doing a shit job of it."

Creed's jaw clenches. "Jesus. We'll get you patched up, brother. I'll call Sparky."

My gut twists. *Why the hell are the Rivet Knights moving against us?*

Blade gasps and grabs Creed's wrist, strength fading fast. "They... they asked about a girl. Called her Jet."

I look up, meeting Creed's eyes.

The same thought hits both of us at once.

*We've got a leak.*

My chest goes cold. *Jet.*

"They know because someone told them," I say flatly.

Then, the first gunshot cracks through the trees.

The brothers scatter for cover, grabbing rifles, yelling orders. Creed is already barking commands. His voice rough and full of authority.

"Lock the gates! Get the women inside!"

I'm running before Creed finishes. Bullets tear into the fence, metal shrieking. I duck behind a truck, return fire, and catch the glint of something moving through the trees near the back gate.

At first, I think it's one of ours circling wide until sunlight catches chrome. It's a bike.

Creeping closer, I find Ronan. He's crouched low, back to me, thumb flying over his phone, and my gut twists.

Keeping low and out of his line of sight, I move silently and fast as the gunfire drowns out my steps.

He glances over his shoulder, and his eyes go wide when he sees me. Ronan drops the phone and reaches for his gun.

*Traitor.*

I close the distance in three strides, grab him by the collar, and yank him backward so hard his feet leave the ground, and the gun skitters from his hand. I throw him down and kick him in the ribs as hard as I can.

"You *stupid* son of a bitch," I snarl. "What the hell did you do?"

He groans, spitting blood. "They have my sister! I didn't have a choice!"

"Bullshit," I growl. "You always have a damn choice."

Now he's crying, shaking like a kicked dog. "I didn't think they'd come this fast—"

"Yeah, well, they did."

A shot ricochets off a tree beside us, so I shove him forward. "You're gonna bleed for this. Creed doesn't tolerate traitors."

My eyes flick to the clubhouse where Jet is located. Every instinct screams to run to her, but Creed's voice cuts through the madness.

"Justice! On me!"

*Duty wins.*

Snatching up Ronan's gun, I fire into his knee. He screams, clutching at the joint, and I know he'll never walk the same. Hell, we both know he won't be leaving the MC alive, not after this. This will keep him down long enough for us to find out who's fucking with the Royal Bastards.

Taking position beside my prez, we keep low and move toward the sound of bikes.

"Time to remind these fuckers whose territory this is," Creed says.

"Couldn't agree more."

We step out from behind cover, side by side.

Gunfire erupts—metal, smoke, blood, chaos.

And just like that, peace dies screaming.

# Chapter 19

## JUSTICE

Gunfire devours the morning. Smoke rolls through the yard, thick with the smell of gunpowder. Shouts echo as bullets tear into the clubhouse.

A truck explodes near the gate, throwing dirt and debris across the compound. Creed barks orders, his voice cutting through the chaos while brothers scramble to cover the perimeter. Every instinct screams one thing...

*Keep them out.*

The Rivet Knights flood the treeline where our back gate should be. Shots crack, engines roar, and the ground vibrates beneath heavy boots.

Creed ducks behind a tree, Glock raised, eyes scanning for a target. He fires, nods at me, and we move ahead, sticking to cover where we can.

A thunderous crash shakes the air as the front

gate folds inward, twisted and smoking. Metal shrieks as a black SUV rolls through the wreckage, tires grinding over gravel.

Not bikes.

Not their style.

The door opens, and out steps Hector Sanchez, calm as ever, suit jacket untouched by the carnage. Two Rivet Knights flank him, weapons drawn.

Creed curses under his breath. "Fucker."

We're pinned down. Can't go back, can't go forward.

Sanchez strolls across the open yard like he owns the place. "Royal Bastards," he calls, voice smooth and smug. "Hell of a morning for a visit."

Creed rises halfway from cover, weapon aimed. "You send men to my gate, you don't get conversation, you get bodies."

A lazy smile touches Hector's mouth. "No need for theatrics. I came for what's *mine*."

"Nothing here belongs to you," I shout back.

"Always the loyal soldier," Hector says, turning toward the sound of my voice. "Didn't realize you'd developed a taste for damaged goods."

Creed and I exchange a confused look.

I shrug, and Creed shakes his head.

"We don't know what you're talking about."

Hector raises his voice, grin widening. "Jet! Get your ass out here before we burn this place to the ground."

"Why Jet?" Creed demands as a bullet hits the tree he's hiding behind.

"Business," Hector replies easily. "The Rivet Knights understand leverage. She's leverage."

"Not anymore." My gun is raised.

The shot tears through the air, slamming into his shoulder. The smirk dies. Then the world detonates, Rivet Knights firing, brothers returning fire, bullets slicing through smoke.

Hector dives behind the SUV as the yard erupts again—metal screams, engines rev—and the war is back in full swing.

Another round hammers into the clubhouse wall. Splinters and brick dust explode around us. Instinct takes over as we drop low, moving behind whatever cover we can find.

Gunfire in the trees suddenly goes silent. I glance up just as a Reaper strolls from the smoke, bloodied, a gun in one hand and a knife in the other. Jogging farther behind him is Winchester.

"Hey, Prez," Reaper says, dark eyes wild. "I went hunting."

Winchester shakes his head. "He's a fucking psycho... but I'm glad he's *our* psycho."

With the threat in the trees cleared, we sprint for the yard just in time to see the black SUV fishtail through the open gate, tires screaming, gravel spitting. The two Rivet Knights inside unload a few last rounds before disappearing down the road.

Creed fires after them until the gun clicks empty, fury boiling off him in waves.

"Where the fuck was everyone?" he roars, spinning toward the brothers. "Who the hell was watching the goddamn gate? And where is *my woman*!"

*Silence.* The kind that stings.

Smoke drifts through the ruined fence. A few of the guys glance at each other, but no one is brave enough to answer.

"Son of a bitch got away," Creed yells, voice raw. "You all see that? Hector Sanchez just walked into our yard, shot up our house, and drove out like he owned the place."

No one moves.

The rage in Creed's voice is enough to strip paint.

I glance toward the clubhouse where Jet's shadow is in the doorway, watching.

My gut twists.

This isn't over.

Not by a long shot.

# Chapter 20

## JUSTICE

Smoke drifts through the wrecked gate. The yard looks like a war zone with bikes on their sides, windows blown out, and blood sprayed across the gravel.

Creed is pacing in the open, gun still in his hand. "Where the fuck was everyone?" he shouts. "Gate duty was covered, so who the hell was covering it?"

No one answers.

A few prospects glance at each other, and one looks ready to puke.

"Get the wounded to the med room," Creed barks. "*Move!*"

Brothers scatter, boots crunching over shell casings. Reaper wipes blood from his cheek with the back of his hand and grins. "Guess we know the Rivet Knights don't scare easily."

Creed rounds on him. "They sure as hell will once I'm done with them." His gaze sweeps the yard, hard and cold, and lands on me. "Ronan's still breathing?"

"Yeah, long as he hasn't bled out. Shot him in the kneecap," I say.

"I'll have him locked in the cage," Winchester adds.

"Good," Creed snaps. "Nobody touches him until I do."

The prez stalks toward the clubhouse, shoulders tight with fury. I fall in behind him.

Devil bursts through the clubhouse doors, tears streaking her face as she launches herself into Creed's arms. He holds her close but doesn't drop his weapon. I can't hear what he whispers, but his eyes are closed, and he buries his face in her neck.

They stay like that for a full minute before Devil slowly pulls back. She nods, wipes her eyes, and disappears inside.

Creed exhales and looks at me. "If anything had happened to her…" He shakes his head and heads inside.

Once upon a time, I wouldn't have understood what he's going through, but now, after Jet?

I get it.

Jet has a piece of my heart, and I think a part of me would die with her.

Inside, the smell of antiseptic fights with

gunpowder. Blake lies pale and half-patched, wincing on a cot while Lucy works fast with gauze and alcohol.

"My dad's on his way," she says, voice tight. "I just need to keep him alive until he gets here."

I nod and keep moving through the clubhouse until I find Jet.

She wraps her arms around me the second she sees me. "He got away, didn't he?"

"Yeah." The word tastes like rust. "Hector's long gone."

Creed slams his fist into the wall, the sound echoing down the hall. "He drove through our front gate like it was nothing! Someone opened that gate, and I'm gonna find out who."

Lyric steps forward carefully. "No one opened the gate. Highway said they used explosives and drove on through after the explosion. We've got wounded, Creed. Maybe—"

Creed whirls on her. "Don't tell me to calm down. One of ours sold us out. Why the fuck do they want Jet? What does she know?"

Jet flinches but doesn't look away. "I... I'm not sure," she says quietly.

"That's not how this works, sweetheart," Creed says, voice still sharp. "He came for you, but he declared war on *us*."

Silence stretches.

Prez looks at me next. "Justice, you're on her

from here on out. Eat, sleep, breathe security. If Sanchez wants her, he'll have to go through you."

"Wouldn't have it any other way."

Creed nods once, then heads for the back hall. "Once I'm done with Ronan, we regroup. We hit back."

He disappears down the corridor, boots heavy on the floorboards.

Jet exhales, the fight draining from her shoulders. "He's mad."

Devil, still staring after her man, shakes her head. "No, love. He's not mad." Her voice drops to a whisper. "He's Creed, president of this chapter, and someone just declared war on his family." Her gaze hardens as she turns toward the yard. "He's not mad, Jet. He's *vengeful*. And that's a whole lot worse."

# Chapter 21

## JUSTICE

The cage sits in the far corner of the clubhouse's garage. It's behind a hidden door. The inside is dark, cold, and reeking of death and blood. It's the club's on-site murder room. It's not something we use often because dealing death in the compound is a recipe for disaster if the local law ever found out.

Only one light burns overhead, a single bulb that flickers every few seconds like it's nervous.

Ronan is inside, slumped against the bars. Sweat glistens on his face, blood pooling beneath his knee. The sweat is from shock, as I'm sure he knows what's about to happen to him.

Winchester is in the cage with him, cleaning the wound, with bandages nearby to wrap it. Creed paces in front of the cage like a predator that hasn't decided if it's going to play or eat.

"Out," Creed says to Winchester without looking at him.

Winchester doesn't argue. He packs up his gear and leaves, closing the door behind him. The air tightens the second he's gone.

"Justice," Creed says, voice low, dangerous. "Lock it."

Clicking the bolt into place, I turn around and look at the man who doesn't have long to live.

Ronan looks up, panic flickering in his eyes. "Prez, I swear—"

"*Don't*," Creed orders. "You don't get to talk yet. You get to listen."

He steps closer, slow and deliberate. "You let Hector Sanchez waltz into my yard, shoot up my brothers, and walk out like it was a Sunday drive."

"I didn't!" Ronan's voice cracks. "They made me! They have my sister—"

Creed slams a hand into the bars. The sound rings like a gunshot. "You think you're the first man to lose family in this life? You think that buys you forgiveness?"

Ronan shakes his head, trembling. "They said they'd kill her if I didn't—"

Creed crouches, eyes level with Ronan's. "And you didn't think to come to *me*?"

Ronan starts to cry, raw and ugly. "I panicked, Prez. I thought I could fix it before it got this far."

Creed's jaw flexes. For a moment, I think he's

going to shoot him right then and there.

Instead, he stands, grabs Ronan by the hair, and forces him to look up. "You didn't just betray *me*, prospect. You betrayed the colors on your back. You got brothers bleeding out there because of you."

Ronan's breathing turns shallow. "I... I didn't know they'd bring Sanchez."

That name makes Creed pause. His grip loosens, but his expression darkens. "You know Hector Sanchez?"

Ronan nods, tears streaking his face. "He's the one who sent the Rivet Knights. Said he's taking back what's his. The Crimson Wheelers were part of it, Prez. They work for him."

A chill runs through the room. The air feels heavier somehow.

Creed looks over at me. "You hearing this?"

"Yeah," I say quietly. "And it makes sense."

Ronan swallows hard. "He said the girl, Jet, belongs to him. That she took something from the Wheelers before she escaped."

Creed's voice turns cold. "What kind of something?"

Ronan shakes his head. "Didn't say. Just that it's worth killing for."

Creed lets go of him and takes a step back, running a hand through his hair. "You just painted a target on every one of us."

"I'm sorry, Prez…"

"Sorry doesn't bring back brothers." Creed's voice drops to a deadly calm. "You'll stay in this cage until I decide what to do with you. And pray the Rivet Knights don't come before I make that call."

He turns to me. "Watch him. I don't want him dead, yet."

Creed leaves, the door slamming behind him.

For a long moment, the only sound is Ronan's ragged breathing.

He looks up at me, eyes full of fear. "They'll kill her, Justice. They'll kill Jet."

My voice is deadly. "Not on my watch."

Ronan's breath rattles in the quiet. For a long second, he merely stares at the bars, then finds me with his eyes and manages a ragged whisper.

"You gotta listen… *please.*" His fingers scrabble weakly at the concrete. "Before they came through, before the Wheelers burned, someone hid a book. They called it a ledger. Names. Routes. Payments. All of it."

"Where?" I ask.

His jaw works. "Toolbox… the mechanic's shed. Under the floorboards. You lift the old red wrench, there's a false bottom. I heard Hector say it. I didn't know what it was… I swear I didn't know."

Cold runs through me. The image stitches itself tightly in my head—a squat shed, engine grease on the floor, a toolbox with a red wrench on top. It's small, stupid, and very specific, yet I remember it. It, like everything else in their compound, was burned to the ground.

"Hector thinks Jet took it," I say. "That's why he's cleaning up loose ends?"

Ronan nods once, eyes hollow. "He'll kill to get it back. He promised. Said he'd bury anyone who stood in the way if his men didn't find it. The Crimson Wheelers weren't as stupid as Hector thought. They had leverage on him, and he didn't even know."

I let the words sit, then stand. The bolt slides home with a hard, measured clank.

Creed is still in the clubhouse. He looks up when I find him in the meeting room, which now looks like a war room. There's a map spread across the table, with coffee cups gone cold, scattered around it.

"He talked," I say without preamble. "Ronan gave a location. The ledger's real. Mechanic's shed at the Wheelers' compound. It was hidden under the floorboards, in a toolbox under a red wrench."

The map flattens beneath Creed's palm. For a beat, there's nothing but the scrape of his hand over the paper. Then he breathes, slow and controlled, and says what I already know.

"We burned it to the ground." His face hardens into the calm that always comes before a storm. "If there was a ledger, it's ash."

"Hector thinks it's real," I say.

Creed nods. "Winchester, Highway, Justice, you go check it out. Maybe something's left. Maybe not." He shakes his head. "But I doubt it."

"Understood," I answer.

Creed looks each of us over. "Be careful. Stick together. And for fuck's sake, if the law's there, keep moving. Don't stop."

"What about Ronan?" I ask.

Creed locks eyes with me. "Reaper and I will handle it. It's not for you to worry about."

For Creed, that's code for, he's as good as dead.

# Chapter 22

## JUSTICE

Jet is sitting on the edge of my bed when I walk in, the morning light cutting through the blinds, making thin, dusty lines across her face. A pistol rests in her lap, hands wrapped around it like it's the only thing keeping her steady.

She looks up when she hears me. "You talked to Creed?"

"Yeah." The word comes out rough. "And Ronan."

Her brows knit. "What did he say?"

Leaning against the wall, I cross my arms, trying to keep my voice level. "It's bad. Worse than we thought."

Her bitter laugh fills the room. "After tonight, I'm not sure what counts as worse."

"The Crimson Wheelers," I start, and her face tightens instantly. "They weren't acting alone, Jet.

**113**

They're working for the Rivet Knights, and Hector Sanchez is bankrolling the whole thing."

She blinks, stunned. "Why?"

Shaking my head, I ignore her question and say, "Ronan confirmed it. The Rivet Knights are his muscle. The Wheelers were his dirty little side project. And you…" My throat tightens, but I force the words out. "You're the last loose end."

The color drains from her face. "Why me?"

"Because you got away. Because you saw too much. And because someone hid something before you escaped."

Her fingers tighten on the gun. "I don't have anything."

"Not on you," I say. "But maybe you know something without realizing it… names, places, conversations? Ronan said Hector's after a ledger the Wheelers kept. It connects him to every illegal deal he's made. When their compound went down, the ledger vanished. He thinks you took it."

Jet shakes her head slowly. "I don't remember any ledger, and you burned it all to the ground."

"Doesn't matter. Hector believes you do."

I take a step closer, lowering my voice. "It's why the Rivet Knights hit us. They're cleaning house for him."

Her eyes fill, not with tears, but with fire. "I'm not running again."

"Good."

The word hangs between us, thick with everything we're not saying. Jet is breathing hard, chest rising and falling like she's bracing for impact. I reach up slowly, brushing a strand of hair from her face. She doesn't pull back.

"You scare the hell out of me," she whispers.

"Yeah," I murmur. "You do the same to me."

Her lips part a fraction, and that's all the invitation I need. I lean in, giving her every chance to stop me. She doesn't.

Our mouths meet, soft at first, then deeper. There's no rush, no demand. Her fingers find my shirt, curling in the fabric, holding on like she's afraid the world might rip us apart.

When the kiss breaks, her forehead rests against mine.

"Justice..." she breathes.

"I've got you," I tell her, my voice low. "No one's taking you from me."

For a moment, there's nothing but the sound of our breathing and the quiet promise that, whatever comes next, we'll face it together.

In the clubhouse, the war room is crowded. Highway, Winchester, Reaper, and the other patched-in brothers are at their places around the table. Jet stands near the door, arms crossed like a shield, watching the room. Creed doesn't waste time.

"Ronan talked," he says. "He confirmed the Rivet Knights are running for Sanchez. The Wheelers were his expendable muscle."

Winchester rubs his jaw. "Sanchez has money. Why use MCs?"

"Because we're expendable," comes the answer. "You use pawns when you don't want blood on your hands."

Clearing my throat, I say, "There were rumors of a ledger. The Wheelers kept it for leverage on Hector, we think." All eyes swivel to me. "We went out there, searched through the rubble. If there was a ledger, the fire took it."

Jet's head snaps up. "So it's gone?"

"Either gone or moved," Winchester says flatly. "Someone wanted it hidden *and* gone."

A heavy silence falls. Creed presses his hands to the table, knuckles white. "What about the women we rescued from the Wheelers?" he asks slowly, looking at Jet. "You weren't the only one they took."

The room leans in while Jet's jaw tightens.

"One of the other girls could have the ledger or at least remember where it went?" I suggest.

A flicker crosses Jet's face. "I remember a girl, her name was Maria. She used to clean for them.

Had access to everything." Her voice goes distant. "I don't know where she went when we escaped."

"Find Maria," Creed says. "Quiet. Fast. If she's alive and knows anything, we need her."

Winchester thumbs his phone. "I'll scan contacts and get Fingers to check his feeds. Fingers and his missus, Nerd, are good at finding people who don't want to be found."

Jet meets my eyes. "Can I help?"

Creed's look is as hard as nails. "No. You don't go out there and get nabbed again. You stay. Justice, make sure she's safe."

Nothing is solved, but a line has been drawn.

The ledger might be ash, or it might be in someone else's hands.

Either way, it's time to start pulling threads.

# Chapter 23

## JET

The war room empties slowly, voices fading down the hallway until it's just Justice and me. He's still standing near the table, arms braced, eyes fixed on nothing.

"You okay?" I ask.

He looks up, and that storm-gray stare hits me like a punch to the chest. "We need to talk," he says quietly. "About your memories."

I nod, even though my stomach twists. The things I remember and the things I don't, they scare me more than bullets ever could.

He leads me down the hall and up the stairs, past locked doors, until we reach his room. He gestures for me to sit, but I don't. I stand close instead, too close, maybe because I want to see what kind of man hides behind that hard jaw and steady voice.

"Close your eyes," he says. "Just breathe. Tell me what you see when you think about the women who were in the Wheelers' compound with you, especially the one you called Maria."

The word alone sends a tremor through me. I shut my eyes. "Maria," I whisper. "She had long dark hair with a gray streak on one side. She had little to do with the other women and me. They let her roam the compound on her own. No guards."

"Could she have been working for the Wheelers?"

My eyes snap open. "But she was in with us."

"Was she really? Or was she there to keep an eye on you all?"

Biting my lip, I nod slowly. "It would make sense."

"What else can you remember about her?"

"She had a tattoo on her wrist, a pair of wings in red, outlined in black."

Justice steps closer, his hand brushing my arm. I breathe him in, and my fingers move before my brain can stop them. I trace the line of his forearm, the muscle flexing under my touch. "Are you always this gentle with witnesses?" I murmur.

He chuckles low, a sound that curls through me and sends a shiver up my spine. "Only the ones who could burn me alive."

We're inches apart. "Careful, Justice," I say, my voice dipping. "You might like the heat."

"I already do."

The air between us crackles. I reach for him again, my fingertips grazing the hollow of his neck, following it down until my knuckles brush the fabric of his shirt. His breath catches, and I feel the restraint in him, the kind that makes a woman want to test every inch of his control.

"Jet." He says my name once, rough and low, as if it's being dragged out of him.

"I'm remembering more," I whisper, but I don't move my hand. "Maria once talked about *Casa del Sol*. It's a Mexican restaurant on Beach Boulevard."

Justice frowns. "Why would you remember that?"

Smiling, I say, "Because I love Mexican food."

I can't stop tracing the ink on his forearm. "You've got your own marks," I say softly. "Guess we both carry ghosts."

His hand catches mine, but instead of pushing me away, he turns my wrist over and presses his lips to the inside. Just once. Just enough to make my knees weak.

"We'll figure this out," he says.

"Okay," I whisper, leaning in so close our breath mingles.

His eyes drop to my mouth, and I swear the world narrows down to that one impossible second before everything breaks. Then his self-control snaps.

Justice grips my hips and pushes me back, guiding me down onto the bed. The mattress dips beneath me as his weight follows, his mouth crashing onto mine in a kiss that's all hunger, heat, and unspoken need. My hands find his shoulders, fingers digging into leather and muscle as his tongue slides against mine, claiming, tasting, and demanding.

The world tilts. The only sounds left are the harsh rhythm of our breathing and the soft drag of fabric as his hand slides along my side. Every brush of his lips feels like a spark catching fire, and every point of contact blurs into one.

When he finally pulls back, his forehead rests against mine, both of us breathing hard.

"You make it difficult to think straight," he mutters, voice rough and low.

"Good." I smile against his lips, still breathless. "Maybe it's time someone else messed with your head for a change."

His laugh is dark and delicious, the sound of control slipping away. And as his gaze searches mine, I realize that for the first time since my release, I'm not afraid.

I'm alive.

"Kiss me like you mean it."

With a low growl, Justice nips my bottom lip and kisses me slowly.

This man knows how to kiss.

He tastes of danger and heat.

His hand travels down my side to my waist, and then he lifts my T-shirt. Justice's fingers lightly graze my bare skin, then he pulls down my bra. His rough hand massages my breast, fingers tweaking my nipple until it pebbles.

My body is betraying every wall I ever built.

The kiss breaks when he stands, boots thudding to the floor like a promise of what's next.

This man is sexy. His body is strong, and his tattoos follow the lines of his muscles. Every mark tells a story, and I want to learn them all.

Justice comes back to me, kissing up my stomach and sucking on my nipple. His tongue flicks across it, and I whimper out, "Justice."

His mouth comes back to mine, fingers digging into my jaw, then his tongue slips past my lips. My hands wrap around the back of his neck.

I don't want this to end.

I don't want him to stop.

*Don't think, Jet, just feel.*

With each stroke of his tongue, my body aches for him. Justice rolls his hips between my legs, and I feel how hard he is through the thin material of my leggings and panties.

My stomach flips and turns, and my nerve endings are on fire, wanting more and more of him.

Rocking my hips against him, I realize this isn't like last time. This is so much better.

Breaking the kiss, I suck on his shoulder and then bite it lightly. He hisses against my neck, so I bite him harder, and he bucks against me.

Justice massages my breast and sucks on my earlobe. His hand slides down the front of my leggings, past my panties, and pushes two fingers inside me.

"You're so wet for me, Jet."

My body arches against him, and I groan.

Justice moves his fingers in and out, stroking the right spot, over and over. I'm lost in him and the sensations he's eliciting from my body.

No fear, only fire.

I'm rocking against his hand, and I'm almost there when Justice stands and pulls my leggings and panties down my legs. Frustrated, I growl at him. "Justice."

He chuckles, cock in his hand, stroking himself, and I swear I've never seen a more manly sight.

"Needy woman."

I nod, and his smile widens.

"Trust me?" he asks.

"Yes," I reply. And I mean it.

This man hasn't hurt me. He's taken care of me. No one has ever asked me to trust them before.

Not like the others.

The Crimson Wheelers, who took what they wanted and never asked. They only hurt me and seemed to relish in that fact.

"Jet, it's just you and me in this room. No one else. Eyes on me, baby. Let me make you feel good."

*Baby?*

*Ooh, I like that.*

Sitting up, I take off my tank top and bra, then scoot farther up the bed.

Justice bends, one hand planted on the bed, eyes locked to mine, and kisses my leg, just below my knee.

"Spread your legs, baby."

Sucking in a deep breath, I do as he asks.

My pulse is a drum, and he's keeping time.

He crawls up the bed, his face inches from my pussy. I should be embarrassed, but Justice makes me feel safe.

"Wider."

Closing my eyes, I bend my knees.

Justice blows on my pussy, and my eyes snap open.

"Better. Keep your eyes on me."

He lowers his head, and his tongue enters me. His hands grip my ass as he laps, sucks, and continues to plunge his tongue inside me.

The tattoos on his shoulders ripple as he continues to work my body into a frenzy.

The orgasm that washes through me as I grind into his face hits hard and fast. I'm helpless as my body shatters, and I feel weightless, floating on the pleasure that rocks through me.

He'll never break me, but with each kiss, touch, and every kind word, he's putting me back together.

Justice stops, positions his cock at my entrance, and slams into me.

He's watching my face, making sure I'm okay. But this is what I need. His cock inside me, Justice slamming into me again and again.

A whimper escapes me as I spread my legs wider for him. He stops and looks down at me.

"Please, don't stop."

Smiling, he lowers himself on top of me, kisses me, and eases himself all the way in again. The hard plains of his stomach feel good against my bare skin, and he thrusts into me faster and faster.

Every thrust steals another piece of my doubt.

Another climax is building. My body is on fire as he hits the right spot, time and time again. The noises I make are nothing short of animalistic as he pounds into me.

*How can something feel this good?*

And then I shatter.

My nails drag down his back, and I clamp down on his shoulder with my teeth. With my body still twitching in pleasure, Justice pulls out and flips me over.

"On your knees."

Wanting more, I do as he says, ass in the air, elbows bent, ready and waiting for him.

"That's my girl."

One of his hands pulls my hair into a ponytail, and he wraps it around his fist. His cock slides into me from behind, his other hand digs into my hip, and he slams into me over and over. Justice lets go of my hair and strokes my clit with deft fingers that apply just the right amount of pressure, and I feel my body is building again.

When his fingers dig harder into my hip, he calls out my name, and I come again.

Justice slams into me one last time and freezes for a moment.

My pussy is throbbing around him, and my only thought is, *is this how it's supposed to be?*

Safe. Wanted. Seen. Cherished.

Justice bends and plants a kiss on my back. "Are you okay?"

A smile creases my face. "Better than okay," I answer.

He thought he'd been rough with me and, like the good man he is, he'd taken care of me. He'd made sure I was fine the entire time, and he didn't come inside me until I'd been sated. It's a rare man who takes care of his woman before he pleases himself.

*His woman?*

My smile grows bigger, *yeah, that's what I am.*

I'm not someone's victim.

I'm someone's choice.

I'm *his*, and Justice is *mine*.

# Chapter
24

## JUSTICE

Winchester is burning whatever he's cooking in the kitchen this morning. The smell of burned bacon fills my nostrils as I make my way downstairs. Creed is sitting at a table, going over a map with Reaper, when Devil walks in, hands on her hips and a look on her face that could scare a god.

"I'm going grocery shopping," she announces.

Creed doesn't even look up. "You don't need to. I'll send a brother."

"The last time you did that, I ended up with twenty cans of beans and enough rice to feed the whole damn state of Florida," she fires back. "We need variety, Creed. Vegetables. Real food."

Reaper snorts. "Beans and rice are real food."

Her glare could melt steel. "You can survive on them then."

127

Creed sighs, rubbing the back of his neck. "Fine. But you're not going alone. Take four brothers with you."

"Deal."

Before anyone else can speak, my hand is already in the air. "I'll go."

Creed's eyes flick to me, sharp and questioning. "You volunteering 'cause you like grocery runs or 'cause you're bored?"

"Neither. Just keeping your ol' lady safe," I answer, tone flat. It's the truth, but it earns me a grunt that sounds halfway between approval and suspicion.

Devil smirks, victorious. "Good. We leave in ten."

Heading down the hall, I find Jet sitting on the couch in the rec room, flipping through a magazine. Her hair is up, a few strands falling against her neck. She looks up, and her eyes brighten when she sees me.

"Going somewhere?" she asks.

"Yeah. Grocery run with Devil and a few of the guys."

"Can I come?"

The question hits out of nowhere. She's been cooped up here since everything went down with the Rivet Knights. For a second, the smart move would be to tell her *no*, to clear it with Creed first, but I don't take the smart move.

"Yeah. Grab your shoes."

She grins, quick and genuine, and something twists in the center of my chest at seeing Jet look so happy. I'd take her on a million runs for groceries if she'd smile at me like that.

The ride to the store is smooth. The late afternoon sun burns low over Jacksonville, orange bleeding into steel-gray. Devil is in the SUV's passenger seat, sunglasses on, muttering about produce. Jet sits behind her, chatting with Coop and Tash. Wrench and Digger follow behind us on bikes, engines rumbling low.

When we pull into the lot, Devil is all business.

"We'll be quick," she says, grabbing a list the length of her arm. "We'll split up to make this quicker. Don't let me catch any of you sneaking beer into the shopping cart."

Her words get a few laughs, even from Jet, and it feels almost normal.

We move through the aisles, putting milk, coffee, and sugar in the cart. The boring shit you forget we actually need to live.

I'm loading a case of water into the trolley when I hear it—raised voices outside—and the sound cuts through the store's hum. Two men are shouting at the back of the store. Something about parking, maybe. The tone's wrong, though.

"Stay with Devil," I mutter to Coop, already heading for the disturbance.

One guy is shoving the other, fake as hell. The

second he spots me, they bolt, splitting in opposite directions.

"Justice!" Wrench shouts. "Outside, white van, left side!"

Sprinting for the front of the store, someone has lit a garbage can on fire at the entrance. I hear squealing but can't see much else through the smoke.

"Jet," Devil screams. "Where's Jet?"

Shoppers scream. Devil is coughing, waving through the haze. Coop is dragging her back. Tash is down, he's bleeding from his side.

My heart stutters. Where *is* Jet?

Moving back inside, I head straight for Devil.

"Time to move!" I bark, grabbing Devil's arm and shoving her toward the door. "*Now!*"

Coop has the SUV in front of the store. Wrench climbs in the back and slides over, as I push Devil into the back of the car. Before we leave, I bend down to check Tash. His eyes are glassy, and there's no pulse.

Scanning the parking lot, there's no sign of Jet.

*Fuck.*

Can't think about it now. Creed's ol' lady is shaking, and the only way we make this right is by staying alive. I climb into the SUV beside her and slam the door shut.

"Devil, head down between your knees," I order.

"What?"

"Until we know it's safe. Do it."

Devil's eyes go wide, but she does as she's told. Digger rides behind us as we speed back to the compound.

The ride is silent except for the engines. Every second stretches like wire, tight and about to snap.

Inside the compound, Creed is waiting at the gates, face carved from granite. Reaper stands beside him, jaw clenched. The second he sees Devil, his shoulders drop, but only slightly.

"She's safe," I manage, voice low, rough. "Jet's gone. Tash didn't make it."

The words hang heavy, like lead.

Before Creed can speak, Winchester storms through the doors, phone in hand, voice tight. "Fingers found her," he says. "Maria. Jet's description nailed it. He's got a fix on her."

"Maria first," Creed snaps. "Jet after. One leads to the other."

Creed puts his hand on my chest and points. "This is on you, brother. Jet shouldn't have left the compound."

He can't make me feel worse than I already do.

I'll burn everything down to get Jet back. "I know."

He nods. "Time to go hunting."

# Chapter 25

## JUSTICE

This part of Jacksonville, on the northern outskirts, feels like a place the world forgot.

Broken fences, burned-out streetlights, it's the kind of neighborhood where every house looks like it's been through a war and lost.

Creed rides point, the rest of us fanning out behind him. Engines snarl through the sticky Florida air, loud enough to rattle windows and make dogs bark in the distance. Gravel crunches under tires as we pull up in front of a sagging, single-story house that's seen better decades.

Paint is peeling, the porch leans to one side, and the yard is a jungle of weeds swallowing a rusted-out Oldsmobile. A beer can glints on the front step.

We kill the engines, and the silence that follows is heavy.

Creed is already off his bike, calm as death. He walks up the steps and knocks once, knuckles sharp against the rotten wood. Then he steps back down into the yard, hands loose at his sides, trying to project he's not a man who could kill them and not lose a minute's sleep.

I'm only hanging on by a thread. My instinct is to pound on that door or kick it in. The woman on the other side is my only lead to Jet. *My Jet.* The woman who's lived through hell and is only just beginning to live again.

For a few seconds, nothing. Then the door groans open, and a man lumbers out. He's overweight, his white shirt covered in brown stains, sweat soaking under his armpits. His jeans hang low, gut spilling over the belt. He stares at the row of bikes and spits into the dirt, then squints at Creed.

"What?"

Creed moves closer one step, but it's enough to steal the man's air. He's in his space, voice low and steady. "Maria."

The man's bravado flickers. His eyes slide over Creed to the line of brothers behind him, Reaper, Winchester, Highway, me, and eleven more. We're a small army, and we take no prisoners.

He backs up a step, looks over his shoulder, and shouts, "Maria!"

A few seconds later, she appears.

Maria is a mess with thin, pale skin stretched tight over sharp cheekbones. Greasy hair pulled into a ponytail, a cigarette burning between her fingers. The tank top she's wearing hangs off one shoulder, revealing bruises that don't look old. Her eyes are ringed in black liner, defiance fighting with fear.

Her gaze jumps from Creed to Reaper, to me, then down again.

She knows who we are.

Knows this isn't a social call.

"Inside," Creed says, and walks straight past her without waiting for an invitation. The man shuffles aside, muttering something under his breath.

We follow Creed in, the door shuts behind us, shutting out the sunlight and the world. The rest of the brothers stay outside, engines idling like wolves waiting at the door.

The smell hits first. It's something of a cross between a wet dog and urine. The floorboards creak under our boots as we move through the cramped living room with a sagging couch and an overflowing ashtray on the coffee table.

Creed stays standing, posture casual, but the calm in him is the kind that hides the storm.

"Maria," he says evenly. "We need to talk about the Wheelers. And a ledger."

She blinks, plays dumb. "Ledger? Don't know what you're talkin' about."

Reaper lets out a low chuckle that makes the hairs on my neck rise.

"That so?" Creed's smirk doesn't reach his eyes, other than to say he is serious. He doesn't have to say anything else.

The tension in the room spikes when Creed tips his chin at Reaper.

Reaper grins, all teeth and menace, and draws his knife. The scrape of steel against leather is slow, deliberate, and fills the room.

Maria's bravado cracks. "Wait! Wait." She holds up her hands. "Don't! Just let me get it."

Creed doesn't blink. "Justice'll help you."

She looks at all of us, and when I move, Maria smiles.

Her fingers tremble as she leads me down a narrow hallway. The air smells stronger of urine. I want to gag or cough, but I keep my features set in a scowl while the carpet squishes under my boots. We stop in a small room lined with warped bookshelves. A single lightbulb hums overhead, flickering.

She moves to a shelf and pulls out an old, large Bible, shaking as she opens it. Inside the hollowed-out pages is another spine. It's the ledger, yellowed with age.

Her voice drops to a whisper. "You don't have to tell them. Hector Sanchez would pay a fortune for this. You and me... we could split it. Be partners."

The audacity makes something inside me snap.

A snarl rips from my throat, and I step in close. "I already have a family, sweetheart." She flinches when I rip the ledger from her hands. "And we don't sell our family."

When I turn back toward the hall, Jet's face flashes in my head—her eyes, that laugh she tries to hide, and my gut twists. Guilt sits like a stone in my chest, heavy and immovable.

Creed and the others are still waiting when I walk back into the living room and hand him the ledger. "Got it."

He takes it without a word, flips it open, and scans a few pages. Whatever he sees there hardens his jaw. "Good work."

We walk out as a unit, the floorboards groaning in relief under our boots. Outside, the fat man is still there, red-faced and sweating. His eyes flick from us to the house.

As we mount our bikes, his voice carries after us. "Maria! What the hell are you doin' in there?"

Engines roar to life, drowning him out.

The ride back to the compound is a blur of headlights and asphalt. Wind rips against my face, but it doesn't clear my head.

Jet is gone because *I* let her go grocery shopping.

Because *I* wanted her close to me.

Every mile feels like punishment.

When we stop, Creed pulls his phone from his

cut, thumb scrolling fast. "Fingers," he says when the line connects, voice low but clear. "Need a number for Hector Sanchez."

A pause, then a lift of his brows. "You've got it already?"

Creed's mouth curves in something that's not a smile. "Good. Text me the number."

It takes only a moment for the text message to appear on Creed's cell phone screen.

He hits call and then waits.

"Hector," Creed says. Calm. Cold. "You've got something of *mine*. I've got something of *yours*. Let's talk."

The silence that follows hums like electricity. Reaper is standing nearby, eyes gleaming. Winchester's jaw works as if he's grinding down his rage.

I stare out into the darkness.

Jet is out there somewhere, scared, alone, and the fault is *mine*.

Creed may be negotiating.

*But me? I'm planning a goddamn war.*

# Chapter 26

## JET

Plastic burns bite the inside of the wrists where the zip ties cut into flesh. The ties looped around a corroded pipe in the ceiling, one of those old plumbing runs, slick with condensation and varnish flakes. My feet dangle inches above a concrete floor, stained dark. Light leaks beneath the door, and I imagine what they are going to do to me.

Last time, terror did the thinking for me. Heart jackhammering. Breath shallow as a trapped bird.

Not tonight.

*Never* again.

Lessons learned the hard way hum along my nerves. I listen to what's happening outside the door, wait for my moment to act, and then I'll move like a blade when the time comes.

Voices in the next room, Spanish, clipped and sounding mean.

One man laughs.

They think they own what's left of me. *They're wrong.*

Blood slicks the plastic, helping the tie to slide. The thing about thick zip ties is that they can cut, but they also loosen once the edge finds its way out. My skin tears and pain blooms like hot metal, but I don't call out.

My bare feet hit the concrete. Muscles scream, but I stay upright. Searching in the dark, I find a chair. The chair feels cheap, so I test its weight. It's heavy enough.

Breathing becomes a tool. Breathe in for three, out for four. Panic will cause me to make a mistake.

No panic.

Not tonight.

*Never* again.

The door opens with a dull thud, bouncing off the other wall. A shadow fills the frame with one man, a gun already moving in his hand. I swing hard. The chair cracks across flesh and bone, shattering into pieces. He doubles over, the firearm jerks free, clattering to the floor.

He will *not* hurt me.

No one is *ever* going to hurt me again.

Bending, I pick up a chair leg and use it like a stake. I slam it into his ribs, and wood splinters dig into my hand. He reaches for me, but I shove him backward with all my might.

The man trips and falls, and I scramble for the gun. Picking it up, I train it on the man on the floor.

The first shot cracks the room open. The sound punches ears, bone-deep. The man's eyes blow wide in surprise, his mouth makes animalistic noises. The second round rips the silence in two, and he doesn't move or make any more noise.

My fingers tremble, my breathing is ragged.

The smell of gunpowder mixes with a copper scent. My hands tremble, but the gun stays level as my chest heaves. No tears. No screams. Just my heartbeat hammering in my ears.

Footsteps outside. Louder this time. Boots, not sneakers.

"Jet!" Justice's voice cuts through the haze.

With a sigh, I let the gun drop to my side. My shoulders sag, and the tension holding me upright loosens for a breath.

He rushes in, eyes wild, taking in the scene.

The body.

The blood.

Then finally, his eyes land on me.

And he's on me before I can speak. Hands gripping my shoulders, sliding down my arms, sweeping over my ribs and waist, fingers shaking as he checks for blood, for holes, for anything that tells him I'm not whole. "You okay?"

A nod, but I am not sure if it's true.

"He was going to—" The words catch in my throat. "I stopped him."

Justice's voice drops, gravel and relief tangled together. "Damn right you did."

The weapon slips from my grasp, landing with a dull thud. Every muscle shakes, but I'm standing.

Still breathing.

Still here.

Not the same woman they took.

Not anymore.

# Chapter 27

## JUSTICE

Smoke pours out of the warehouse as the fire eats everything behind us. The heat licks at my back, the air thick and bitter with ash and burned oil. Jet's body trembles in my arms, blood smeared across her face and tangled in her hair. She's as light as a feather, and yet every step feels heavy, like I'm carrying the weight of my own failures with her.

Her head rests against my chest, breaths shallow but steady. Every breath reminds me she's *alive* and that word alone feels like a miracle.

"You did good, baby," I murmur, voice rough from smoke and emotion I can't swallow. "You're safe now."

Her fingers twitch weakly against my cut, and it damn near breaks me.

Behind us, Reaper and Winchester watch the

flames clean up the mess, making sure nothing and no one walks away from this.

Brotherhood at work—it's silent, precise, and deadly.

Creed's voice cuts through the chaos. "Pull out. It's time to go. We're done here."

*Done.*

If only my conscience believed that.

By the time the bikes roar down the highway, night has started to fade. Jet is wrapped in my jacket, huddled against me in the truck. Her hands tremble when she tries to wipe her face, so I do it for her. Every bruise is a reminder of what could have been.

God, the thoughts that crawl through my head, what those bastards might have done if she hadn't fought back, turn my stomach.

I keep glancing over, making sure she's still breathing. Still here. Still with me. But I can't shake the image of her standing there with a gun in her hands, shaking but defiant, blood on her face, fire in her eyes.

She's the bravest woman I've ever known.

And I almost lost her.

The drive feels like it takes forever, but finally, back at the clubhouse, it feels like the world stops moving.

I carry her through the clubhouse, ignoring the looks from the brothers, the questions in their eyes.

She's *mine* to protect.

Always will be.

The door to my room shuts behind us with a quiet click, cutting off the club's noise.

She sits on the edge of the bed, hair falling around her face, hands fisting the blanket. When her gaze lifts to mine, it's full of exhaustion and something sharper.

"How did you find m-me?" Her voice cracks. "How did you know where I was?"

Leaning against the dresser, I scrub a hand down my face. "Creed made a deal. Traded the ledger for your location."

She stares, disbelief clouding the fear. "So he got away with it? Hector?"

A faint smile tugs at my mouth—grim, humorless. "For now. But Hector's the kind of man who always circles back. And when he does, he'll get what's coming."

Her shoulders sag. A tear slips free and tracks down her cheek. I cross the room and drop to my knees in front of her. My hands find hers, cold and trembling.

"Jet," I whisper. "I'm sorry."

Her eyes lift, uncertain.

"I shouldn't have let you come with us. Should've kept you safe, kept you here, away from all this shit." My voice breaks, and I swallow hard. "You could've been killed... or lost to me. And I wouldn't

**144**

have been able to live with that. I love you, Jet. I love you more than I've ever loved anything in my damn life."

Her breath catches. Eyes wide, wet, disbelieving. "You... *you* love *me*? But you're perfect, and I'm—"

"*No.*" The word comes out rough, cutting through her doubt. "You're the one I want. The one I love. The one who makes me want to be better. You're *everything*, Jet."

Silence stretches between us, heavy and raw. Then her fingers tighten around mine.

Tears shimmer in her eyes, but her voice is steady when she whispers, "I love you too. More than I ever thought I could. Life's full of danger, Justice... yours, mine, everyone's, but if we've got each other's backs, we'll be fine."

A shaky laugh escapes me. "You sure about that, baby? 'Cause I don't ever wanna feel what I felt when you were gone."

She leans in, forehead resting against mine. "You won't have to. I'm right here, and I'm not going anywhere."

When our lips meet, it's slow, nothing like the hunger that usually drives us. This is something else. Something honest. A promise made in silence and sealed with tears.

Her hand slides up to the back of my neck, and for the first time since that van took her, the knot in my chest loosens. The world outside could burn, and I wouldn't care.

I hold her close, whisper against her hair, "I've got you, Jet. Always."

And as she breathes against me, soft and steady, one truth roots deep in my chest.

*I'm the luckiest bastard alive.*

# Chapter 28

## JET

Weeks pass in a haze of healing. My scabs are fading, the bruises are turning from purple to yellow to pale shadows. However, the internal scars are something else.

They don't fade.

The nightmares come and go, flashes of that night bleeding into dreams. Sometimes it's the sound of the gunshot. Sometimes it's the smell of smoke. But every time, I wake up to the same thing—Justice's hand wrapped around mine, his chest rising and falling steadily beside me.

He hasn't left my side. Not once.

Part of me is grateful. The other part, the one that's used to surviving alone, feels the edges of panic. I hate feeling dependent, weak, or needing anyone.

This morning, sunlight creeps through the blinds, cutting across the bed in golden slashes. Justice is sitting in a chair near the window, boots propped on the dresser, coffee mug in hand. He looks at me as if I'm the only thing that matters.

"I'm not broken, you know," I say quietly. "I just need to figure out what I'm going to do with the rest of my life."

He sets the mug down and leans forward on his knees. "You're not broken, Jet, and you're not alone. You're the strongest woman I know. What you went through? What you did to survive? It would have destroyed most people."

The truth in his voice hits somewhere deep, and my throat tightens.

"I just don't want to be the reason you stop living," I whisper. "You've got your brothers, the club, a whole damn life outside this room. And I need to find a life too."

He stands, steps close, and cups my jaw, thumb brushing my cheek. "You *are* my life now. The rest? It's just noise."

Creed came to me last week with an offer, not charity, but a genuine job. The club owns a few strip joints across Jacksonville, and their books are a mess. Numbers never scared me, so now I handle the accounts, payroll, and licensing. Creed said if the brothers trust me with their money, I'm part of the family. It feels good to work again, to have something that's mine, something that keeps me sharp.

Tonight, the whole club gathers out back with a giant bonfire blazing, smoke curling into the stars. Laughter cuts through the music, but when Creed steps forward, everything quiets.

Justice stands beside me, hand linked with mine, his thumb tracing circles on my skin.

Creed's voice carries across the fire, deep and commanding. "Jet, you've stood where most would've fallen." He pauses, his gaze shifting to Justice before coming back to me. "The man at your side has something he wants to ask you, and he's got my blessing."

My heart pounds. The brothers watch, silent and respectful.

Creed nods toward Justice.

"Tonight, she's claimed." Justice squeezes my hand, eyes locked on mine. "You're *mine*, baby. My ol' lady. My heart."

Emotion clogs my throat. There's no fear this time, only certainty. "*Yours*," I say, voice steady.

Creed steps closer, the firelight turning his face to bronze and shadow. "Then she gets a name worthy of what she's survived."

He looks straight at me. "From this night forward, you're *Phoenix.* You rose from the ashes of your past life and built a new one in blood, fire, and danger. But it's yours now, earned in pain, forged in strength, and protected by this brotherhood."

The brothers roar in approval, the sound echoing into the night.

Justice pulls me close, his lips against my ear. "Phoenix," he murmurs. "Fits you, baby. Strong. Beautiful. Untouchable."

My chest swells with something fierce and alive. The fear that once chained me is gone.

Around me, the flames crackle, the brothers cheer, and Justice's arm stays firm around my waist.

For the first time since everything fell apart, I finally believe what Creed said.

I *did* rise from the ashes.

And this life—the danger, the love, the chaos— it's *mine* now.

# Chapter 29

## CREED

Heelz, our strip club, is quiet this time of night. It's perfect for meetings. No one here will bother us, and it gets swept for bugs daily.

The girls aren't out yet. It's just the soft shuffle of movement backstage and the low pulse of bass through the floor. The air smells like whiskey, sweat, and cheap perfume.

Lev Ivanov sits across from me in the private booth at the back, jacket draped across the seat, shirt crisp enough to slice skin. He's got that polite smile, one that never reaches his eyes, the kind only a man born into power can pull off.

I slide a folded photocopy folder across the table. It's the ledger.

He looks down at it, fingers tapping the edge. "And why show me this, Creed?" Lev asks. "You don't strike me as a man who shares his toys easily."

I take a slow drink of bourbon before answering, "Hector Sanchez took a woman under my protection. Her name's Jet. Hector thinks he can trade her for that ledger. I'm meeting him later tonight."

Lev glances up. "Why are you telling me this?"

"Because I know what's in it." I lean forward slightly, lowering my voice. "It's got every name Hector's been working with... suppliers, dealers, transport routes. Some of those names might interest you."

A flicker of amusement ghosts across his face as he unfolds the copy, scanning a few lines. "They do indeed." He looks up again, eyes glinting. "What do you want?" Lev leans back, resting an arm across the booth. "And this girl... is she worth all this trouble?"

"She's under the club's protection," I repeat. "That makes her worth it. And one of my men wants her back."

He studies me for a long moment, then smiles. "Tell me, who is the member who would risk this much?"

"Justice," I reply.

Lev's grin widens. "Ah. The quiet one. I have heard of him. Perhaps he would like to be there when we... handle this Hector problem?"

I smile back, slow and deliberate. "Yeah. I think he'd like that just fine."

Lev raises his glass, and I match it. Crystal meets crystal, two devils toasting the cost of keeping what's theirs.

The next night, the rain hasn't stopped all day.

Justice and I follow one of Lev's men through a narrow hallway that smells like bleach, and where plastic lines the floor. Igor, a big bastard, shaved head, arms covered in faded ink, leads us down a concrete staircase into the bowels of a basement.

The basement has a spotlight shining on Hector Sanchez. His eyes are closed, and he hangs in the same way he had Jet hanging, with thick plastic ties cutting into his wrists, sweat and blood dripping from his face. His expensive shirt is torn open, the arrogance gone, replaced by a sickly kind of panic.

Igor opens the door, nods once, and steps aside. Then he's gone, leaving the three of us alone.

Hector starts talking the second the door closes. "Creed, listen to me, brother, this wasn't personal. I can make this right. Whatever you want… money, product, women, anything!"

His words bounce off the walls, desperate and frantic.

Justice stands beside me, silent, hands flexing at his sides. I feel the storm in him, the tension, the weight of what Jet went through.

Hector's voice cracks. "Please. I can help you. We can work together—"

Justice steps forward, slow and steady, until he's inches from Hector's face. His voice is low, cold enough to freeze the air between them. "I should make you suffer. Drag this out. Watch you bleed for it." He pauses, eyes narrowing. "But it's not my call."

I say nothing. Just nod once.

Justice raises his gun. The sound is deafening in the small room, one sharp, final crack.

Hector's body jerks once, then goes limp, hanging by the wrists like a broken marionette. Fragments of bone and brain matter spray outward, a violent bloom against gray. Blood splatters across the wall, hot and thick, painting the concrete in dark streaks.

For a long moment, the only sound is the slow drip of blood hitting the floor.

Justice lowers the gun, his breath ragged. When he turns toward me, his jaw is tight, eyes shadowed but clear. "Debt's paid."

I nod. "Yeah. It is."

He looks at me again, voice low. "Thank you for letting me end him."

"Don't thank me, brother," I say, meeting his stare. "Just remember why we did it, not only for Jet, but for the club and for what's ours."

He nods once solemnly, and together we walk out, the sound of our boots echoing through the concrete hall.

Behind us, Hector Sanchez hangs in silence, another ghost swallowed by the darkness that made him.

Outside, the night air hits cold and clean for the first time in a long while. He was named Justice as he has his own brand of it, and tonight he lived up to his name.

Jet will never know what he did.

This is Royal Bastards' business, but the brothers will know.

And most of all, so will Justice.

# Chapter 30

## CREED

The Rivet Knights are a thorn in our side, but they've gone underground. Fingers and his ol' lady, Nerd, are on it, but so far, nothing. Either they have left Jacksonville, or they're plotting to hit back at us, but without Hector Sanchez bank-rolling them, I'm leaning toward ran. We've got chapters all over the country, and I've sent word out that I'm looking for them. They're a small club, maybe thirty men, and numbers matter. That's why they don't stand a chance.

I sit outside, watching my woman and Jet in the redneck pool. They're drinking Fireball out of plastic cups, sunk in the back of a truck that's been lined with a tarp so the water stays put. Music is playing, Devil keeps hitting replay on The Grinders' song, "Heaven." I swear I'm about ready to shoot her phone or the Bluetooth speaker if she plays that damn song one more time.

"Yo, Prez!" Winchester is coming toward me, phone held over his head like a flag.

"What?" I say, not taking my eyes off my woman as she laughs.

"Rock, president of the Durango, Colorado chapter, wants a word." He hands me the phone.

"Winchester, what are you doing answering my phone?" I ask.

He shrugs. "It rang. You weren't around, so I answered it." He walks off like I'm the idiot.

"We aren't done," I call after him. He flips me the bird without looking back. Then he sighs and stops.

I put the phone to my ear. "Rock? It's Creed. How goes it?"

"Moving and shaking, trying to earn a living. You?"

"Good, man. Sun's shining. I'm relaxing in the shade with a cold one, watching my woman in a bikini."

"Still with that little Aussie?"

I chuckle. "Yeah, Devil. She's a handful. What can I do for you?"

"Is this a clean line?"

"No."

Rock makes a noise that sounds like sucking air through his teeth. "Can you ring me back on a clean line?"

"A little paranoia never did anyone harm. Give me a minute." I end the call, finish my beer, and stroll over to Devil.

"Hey, babe." She leans up and kisses me.

"Have you got sunscreen on?" I ask.

She rolls her eyes. "I come from the skin cancer capital of the world. Of course, I have sunscreen on."

"Don't stay out too long."

"Party pooper."

"Maybe I want a different kind of party?" A wicked grin splits her face, and she looks at me softly. "I could get out now," she says.

"Gotta make a call, but I'll see you in thirty."

"Okay, honey." She kisses me again. She tastes like Fireball, and I playfully bite her lip. "Half an hour."

Jet laughs. "That was hot."

"Yeah, and he's *all mine*." They both burst out laughing.

Winchester is still waiting when I walk by. "Come with me," I tell him.

"Aww, shit, Creed. It's just a phone. I only answered it."

Ignoring him, I head for the meeting room. "Take a seat." I scan the clubhouse until I find Reaper, who's staring at me. With a tilt of my head, I gesture for him to join us. Lucy is on his lap, talking to Highway. He slaps her ass, she stands, yelps, and rubs it.

"You're an ass, you know that?" she snaps.

Reaper smirks. "Yeah, babe. I know, and you love it." He saunters over with Lucy glaring daggers at his back.

"Why does she stay with you?" I ask.

"It's my winning personality," he says, sitting at the table. I close the door and take my place at the head. Winchester folds his arms and raises an eyebrow. "Seriously? You're so pissed I answered your phone, we're having a meeting about it?"

"You answered his phone?" Reaper asks.

"It was ringing."

"Even I wouldn't answer his phone."

Winchester huffs, and I shake my head. "Rock rang and needed a clean line. I came in here, where we have burners, and figured you'd both want to hear what he wants."

Reaper laughs as I dial Rock back and put the call on speaker.

"Creed?"

"Yeah, Rock. What gives?"

"We're working a deal to sell a great deal of guns to a buyer out of Florida and need you to check him out. It's a lot of hardware, but we need to know if he's legit."

"We can do that. Text me what you've got, and I'll have my boys run him."

Winchester clears his throat. "Rock, is Memphis

still with you?"

"Yeah, man. Looks like he's staying."

"Met him in New Orleans once, had a hell of a time with him during Mardi Gras. Glad he found a place to settle." Rock chuckles. "Sounds like him. I'll shoot you the info."

"We're on it," I say and end the call.

"Guns?" Reaper asks. "With all the heat on us, should we be near that?"

"We're not in it, only vetting. You and Winchester check it out."

"And what are you going to do?"

I wink. "Spending time with my ol' lady."

"So you get pussy duty, and we have to work?" Reaper shakes his head.

"After what you did to Lucy, don't expect any for a while," I tell him. He looks at Lucy, and she gives him the finger. "Try apologizing. And chocolate, Devil loves chocolate, but not ours. She wants that stuff from New Zealand... costs me a fucking fortune."

"Why get it then?" Winchester asks.

"Because she likes it."

Moving out of the room, I head to our room. Devil is fast asleep, wet hair fanned on the pillow, her skin still warm from the sun. She's beautiful when she's dead to the world, one arm thrown over my side of the bed like she owns it. I lean down and kiss her temple. She tastes like Fireball, sunscreen, and sin. For the first time in weeks, the weight in my chest eases.

The club is running smoothly.

Jet is healing.

Justice finally smiles again.

For now, everything's quiet.

But quiet never lasts long in this life. The Rivet Knights may be hiding, but ghosts don't stay buried. And with Rock calling about gun deals out of Florida... yeah, peace never lasts long.

I pull off my cut, climb into bed beside my woman, and wrap an arm around her. She stirs and murmurs, "You smell like trouble."

A slow grin curls my lips. "Always do, baby."

Then I close my eyes, knowing the storm is coming.

And that's when it hits, the Royal Bastards will be ready to face it head-on.

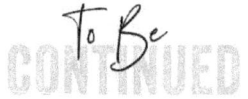

The road doesn't end here!

Pick up

**Open Road**

The Royal Bastards MC, Jacksonville, Florida

https://readerlinks.com/l/5140665

More Royal Bastards MC titles await below:

Creed Book 1
Reaper Book 2
Highway Book 3

# More books
## TO CHECK OUT

**The Savage Angels MC Series**

Savage Stalker Book 1
Savage Fire Book 2
Savage Town Book 3
Savage Lover Book 4
Savage Sacrifice Book 5
Savage Rebel (Novella) Book 6
Savage Lies Book 7
Savage Life Book 8
Savage Christmas (Novella) Book 9
Savage Release Book 10
Savage Heart Book 11
Savage Angels Book 12
Savage Angels MC Collection Books 1 – 3
Savage Angels MC Collection Books 4 – 6
Savage Angels MC Collection Books 7 – 9
Savage Angels MC Collection Books 1 - 9

Kathleen Kelly

## The MacKenny Brothers Series
An MC/Band of Brothers Romance

Spark Book 1
Spark of Vengeance Book 2
Spark of Hope Book 3
Spark of Deception Book 4
Spark of Time Book 5
Spark of Redemption Book 6
Spark of Passion Book 7
Spark: MacKenny Brothers Series Books 1 - 3

## The Tackling Series
Tackling Love Book 1
Tackling Life Book 2

## Standalones
Wraith
Fealty: A Wraith Novel
Cardinal: The Affinity Chronicles Book 1
Snake's Revenge: Gritty Devils MC

# Connect With
## ME ONLINE

Check these links for more books from
Author Kathleen Kelly

## READER GROUP

Want access to fun, prizes and sneak peeks?
Join my Facebook Reader Group.
https://bit.ly/32X17pv

## NEWSLETTER

Want to see what's next?
Sign up for my Newsletter.
https://www.subscribepage.com/kathleenkellyauthor

## BOOKBUB

Connect with me on Bookbub.
https://www.bookbub.com/authors/kathleen-kelly

Kathleen Kelly

# GOODREADS
Add my books to your TBR list
on my Goodreads profile.
http://bit.ly/1xsOGxk

# AMAZON
Buy my books from my Amazon profile.
https://amzn.to/2JCUT6q

# WEBSITE
https://kathleenkellyauthor.com/

# TIKTOK
https://www.tiktok.com/@kathleenkellyauthor

# TWITTER
https://twitter.com/kkellyauthor

# INSTAGRAM
https://instagram.com/kathleenkellyauthor

# EMAIL
kathleenkellyauthor@gmail.com

# FACEBOOK
https://bit.ly/36jlaQV

# About THE AUTHOR

**Kathleen Kelly is a *USA Today* and International Best-Selling Author,** known for her fast-paced, spicy romance novels. She writes MC, Paranormal, Sports, and Band of Brothers Romance. When she's not writing, she's collecting handbags (they always fit!) and planning her next international trip.

Living in Toowoomba, Queensland, with her childhood sweetheart, SL, rescue cat Freya, and Eir, a Maine Coon with main-character energy, Kathleen values kindness, loyalty, and good stories.

Kathleen loves hearing from readers and can easily be found on Facebook.

If you have any questions about her novels or would like to ask Kathleen a question, she can be contacted via email:

kathleenkellyauthor@gmail.com

or she can be found on Facebook. She loves to be contacted by those that love her books.